A log shifted on the fire, sparks shot into the air, burned bright and disappeared.

"I want to feel you against my skin," Megan murmured, as her tongue caressed Randall's ear. She pulled Randall's sweater off in one continuous movement, then slid other clothing over Randall's hips, letting it fall in a soft heap on the floor.

Randall watched with mounting desire as Megan removed her own sweater. She reached up and traced the firelight already caressing Megan's breasts. Megan stood, and let the rest of her clothing fall from her body.

For a moment time was frozen for Randall. Spellbound by the strength of her own desire, she caressed Megan's body with her eyes. Then she felt the pliant softness of their flesh come together as Megan's body covered hers completely. The fresh scent of Megan's skin overwhelmed her senses. Desire spun in her brain like a child's top gone wild. Randall knew only the barest sensation of weight as Megan brushed her skin with her own.

So this is how a woman feels. A passing thought as she closed her eyes, as she reached up and pulled Megan firmly against her, and fell into her own pleasure.

CHERISHED
LOVE

BY EVELYN KENNEDY

CHERISHED
LOVE

BY EVELYN KENNEDY

NAIAD
1988

Printed in the United States of America
First Edition
Edited by Katherine V. Forrest
Cover design by The Women's Graphic Center
Typesetting by Sandi Stancil

Library of Congress Cataloging-in-Publication Data

    Kennedy, Evelyn, 1939—
       Cherished love / Evelyn Kennedy.
       p. cm.
    ISBN 0-941483-08-8 : $8.95
    I. Title.
    PS3561.E4263C5 1988   87-31184
    813'.54--dc 19   CIP

For Betty
Happy Eighteenth Anniversary.

If I had to choose again —
I would still choose you.

About the Author

Evelyn Kennedy brings a varied background to the art of fiction. She spent several years as a cloistered nun, completed a tour of duty as a paramedic with the military, taught on the University and Nursing School level, holds a brown belt in Karate, writes poetry for her own enjoyment, and admits to being an incurable romantic. This is her first novel.

C H E R I S H E D
LOVE

BY EVELYN KENNEDY

Chapter 1

Dr. Megan McKenzie left Emory Hospital at three o'clock, having spent the morning in surgery and the afternoon lecturing to residents about coronary by-pass procedures. She held a permanent position on Atlanta's only heart transplant team, and in three years had assisted in three successful transplants, in addition to maintaining a large private practice in cardiology, and serving as guest lecturer at the medical school and its affiliated hospitals.

She was dark-haired and attractive, with pale gray eyes that caught people with a glance and held them without effort. After ten years in medical practice, her gentleness and sensitivity surprised anyone who expected a top-flight cardiologist to be more scientist than human being. She had learned the secret that allowed her to be both — an elegant truth she had lived since childhood: she was herself in all situations. No masks, no roles, just plainly and simply herself.

As a physician, Megan had declared war on death, had made it her personal enemy. Her waking hours were dedicated to repairing hearts that would otherwise doom their owners to an early death. She threw herself into the war with the intensity of a mother battling for the life of her child. She had not always won the battles, and she had never learned to lose gracefully.

Megan started dinner shortly after arriving home. Dinner meant heating or microwaving whatever she had purchased from a take-out gourmet shop. Her lover Ellen had often teased that it was a good thing Megan was better with a scalpel than she was with a saucepan. Megan had always countered that she had had better teachers in surgery than in cooking.

At 5:45 there was a knock on the door. "I'm Officer Collins, with the Atlanta Police Department. Is Dr. McKenzie at home?"

"I'm Dr. McKenzie." She looked at the uniformed, grim-faced young officer with concern but not alarm; his visit undoubtedly had to do with some patient of hers.

"May I come in?"

"Certainly."

Removing his hat, he seated himself in a chair in the living room, and held his hat in the fingers of both hands as he waited until Megan sat down on the sofa.

"Doctor, I'm afraid I have bad news for you." For an instant his gaze dropped from hers and there was silence; then he continued, "There's been a very bad accident. Dr. Klein's car was hit head-on by a van."

Megan's heart lurched. "Is she hurt badly? What hospital did they take her to?"

"I'm sorry, Doctor." The young officer's voice was calm. "She was pronounced dead at the scene."

Megan received the words like a physical blow. She fought to focus her eyes as the room began to spin slightly. The officer went on quietly with details of the accident.

"Where is she?" Her tone was even.

"They took her to St. Joseph's Hospital."

"I understand."

"I'm terribly sorry." He looked at her with earnest blue eyes. "Would you like me to remain for a while, doctor — perhaps until you call a friend to be with you? May I drive you somewhere?"

"You're very kind," Megan said automatically. "But I'll be all right." She rose, and he obediently followed her to the door. "I appreciate your courtesy, Officer."

So this was what it was like to receive the news of a loved one's death, she thought numbly as she closed the door after him. She had been the bearer of that news on many occasions, announcing to family members or friends that a parent, a child, a spouse, a lover had died. Now she stood in that place herself. The major element in her life, her most significant other, was gone. Ellen Klein, a woman who had spent her life helping others, who was working on a major breakthrough in heart disease, had been destroyed by a drunken construction worker, arrested only six months earlier for DUI. He had been fined five hundred dollars, then sent back on the road. He wouldn't be driving again — but neither would Ellen.

Megan dialed Lynn Bradley's number. She began talking, faintly aware that her voice seemed to come from far off, aware that she was separating herself from her words.

* * * * *

3

Lynn Bradley was with Megan when she saw Ellen's body. It was Lynn who arranged for the funeral home, who took Megan to her own home for the night.

Sitting at Lynn's kitchen table, Megan said, "I have to call Bob Southerby and ask him to cover for me." She was running on automatic pilot. "I have a by-pass in the morning."

"I've already called for you." Lynn placed a cup of coffee in front of Megan. "Would you rather have a drink? Bob will take your surgery and your office schedule."

"Do you have any Jamison's? I could use some."

Lynn got the Jamison's and poured a large amount into Megan's coffee.

"I can't believe this, Lynn. I can't believe my whole life can change in a matter of minutes." She wiped away the tears from her cheek. "I don't know what I'll do without Ellen."

"You'll go on with your practice just as Ellen would want you to do. You'll hurt and you'll miss her terribly, but you will go on. Eventually the pain will be gone, and you'll still be here." Lynn smiled briefly. "Remember, I speak from experience."

Megan reached out and patted Lynn's hand. "I know you do. I don't know how you got through it. I need your secret now." Megan took a long drink from her cup.

Lynn squeezed Megan's hand. "There is no magic. We hang in and endure. Joyce would have wanted that for me, and I know Ellen would want it for you."

"Wise words from a psychiatrist," Megan said heavily.

"They're words from a friend who loves you and Ellen very much. We've been friends for a long time, Meggie. I know you, and I know the pain you feel and will feel in the future. I wish I had some kind of magic for you, something that would make it all better."

Lynn took a swallow of her coffee. She poured more Jamison's into Megan's cup along with some fresh coffee.

"I thought I would die when I found out Joyce had lung cancer. Then when she died I was afraid — because I knew I'd have to stay here without her and somehow make it through the pain." Her eyes reflected that pain for an instant. "If there was ever a classic case of physician heal thyself, I was it. I'd worked with hundreds of patients through grief — but when it was my grief, my loss, my lover who was dead, all the training, all the diplomas on the wall didn't mean a thing. All I knew was, the person who meant more to me than anyone on the planet was gone. I couldn't call her at noon to say hello, I couldn't meet her for a quick lunch, I couldn't stop what I was doing at home and hear her moving about in some other part of the house. I couldn't reach to her and touch her, I couldn't tell her what had happened that day, or what shape my hopes and dreams were taking. There are no words for the pain. It was as though a large, dull knife had cut through everything soft inside me, had left me empty."

She reached over to Megan, wiped a tear from the corner of her eye. "Meggie, I know it hurts, but you'll make it. The bad news is there will be many times when you'll feel the pain even more than you do now — you have shock on your side at this moment — but when those times come, you'll still make it through. And Meggie, I'll be there for you. Just as you and Ellen were there for me."

In accordance with Ellen's wishes, she was buried from the Cathedral of Christ the King following a Requiem mass. Lynn got a colleague to take her own patients and spent the next two weeks with Megan, helping her sort through Ellen's personal things and being generally available. Megan stayed at Lynn's house for three weeks before she returned home. Even then, Lynn was a nightly visitor for dinner or invited Megan to her house. Gradually Megan ate more dinners alone or with other colleagues or friends. Gradually she fell out of the habit of talking to Lynn every day. Lynn was there if she needed her, and that was enough.

Chapter 2

In the thirteen months after Ellen's death Megan increased her patient load. In addition to performing surgery twice a week, she also donated two afternoons each week at a free clinic. She had all but volunteered herself into the position of regular on-call physician for her medical group. Her partners knew they could count on her to take their on-call time whenever any inviting situation presented itself.

By her own design, she had submerged herself in her work. Somehow she felt close to Ellen while examining a patient or performing surgery, making use of the skills and art Ellen had taught her. She could imagine Ellen's voice: "All right, Megan, you hear the murmur, you have the results of the blood work, what's your prognosis?" Medicine, cardiology, was a place where she and Ellen still lived together.

Megan's social life involved lunch or dinner with Lynn once or twice a week. She saw other friends rarely, and she had given up completely the cocktail parties she had never liked. It was Ellen who had always insisted that minimum attendance at certain events was a political necessity. Since Ellen's death, the only necessity Megan recognized was the practice of medicine.

Along with the unopened mail at home, Megan had completely ignored phone messages concerning financial investments that she and Ellen had made together and so she was not at all surprised when her secretary informed her that Randall Grayson, an attorney with Hodges, Stevens, and Murray was on the phone, demanding to speak with her.

"Get his name and number and I'll call him back," Megan said uninterestedly.

"*Her* name," the secretary said. "She said to tell you that you could lose a lot of money if you don't talk to her today."

"Okay, I'll take the call." Irritated, Megan punched the flashing button. "This is Dr. McKenzie. What do you need?"

"It's not what *I* need, Doctor, it's what *you* need," a woman's voice said calmly. "You're a difficult person to contact. Didn't you get my letters?"

"I don't recall any specific letters at the moment," Megan said, picturing the stack of unopened mail in her study at home. "What is it I need?"

There was a chuckle. "I'd say you needed a full-time secretary at home," the woman said. "You have investment property that needs your attention. We need to get together on this by Wednesday."

"I think one of your firm's other attorneys handles all that. Can't you check with him?"

"Not really, Doctor. He moved to Vermont about three months ago. Seems the difficulty he had getting in touch with certain clients wore on his nerves. The files were turned over to me two months ago. That's when I sent you the first letter." The lawyer paused briefly. "I know you're busy, Doctor, but if I'm going to do your real estate investments justice, I do need to meet with you. We're talking a lot of money here — your money."

"I'm scheduled all day." Megan looked at the appointment calendar on her desk. "I'm not free until five-thirty. Tomorrow I'm in surgery until one o'clock and have appointments until six."

"I'll take today at five-thirty," the lawyer said. "I'll look for you then."

"Where are you located?" Megan asked.

"Doctor, I'm beginning to believe your heart is not in real estate investments. Have you never been here before?"

"No, my partner took care of most of our investments. I never had occasion to go to your office." Megan paused. "I'm afraid I don't have a very good head for business."

"Well, your partner, Dr. Klein, made some very wise investments for you."

In her office high above Peachtree Road, the phone wedged between her shoulder and ear, Randall Grayson leafed through the file folder on her desk. The file listed real estate holdings worth more than one and a half million dollars. She fingered a copy of the death certificate and the letter notifying the firm that Ellen Klein was dead.

"I'm sorry about your partner. I never met her, but I know she had a good business sense." Randall didn't know what else to say about this client's death. She had no idea what Dr. McKenzie might be feeling. Doctors weren't like regular people; they dealt with death all the time. After all, they lost patients every day.

"Look," Randall said, "I have to be out your way about five o'clock. How would it be if I came by your office?"

"That would be a lot more convenient for me," Megan replied.

"Fine. And by the way, we're in Lenox Towers, right across from the Lenox Square Mall. Just for future reference."

"I'll keep that in mind," Megan said in an amused tone. "I'll see you this afternoon."

Again Randall leafed through the file. Her mind was asking questions that didn't involve real estate. Nothing in the file indicated that the two women were related. Klein was fifteen years older than McKenzie. Maybe they were related through marriage — or maybe . . . Randall picked up the file, shrugged into her navy suit jacket, and walked down the hall to Tom Jordan's office.

"Tom, you worked on the Klein-McKenzie file before. Ever meet them?" Randall took a chair across from Jordan.

Tom Jordan took off his glasses and rubbed his hands over his gray satin-backed vest. "I met Dr. Klein several times. A very bright lady. Has a sixth sense about real estate investments."

"Had a sixth sense," Randall said slowly. "Dr. Klein was killed about thirteen months ago. Dr. McKenzie is now sole owner of all the holdings. I just got off the phone with her. She didn't even know where our office is located. She doesn't sound too interested in business."

Jordan leaned back in his chair. "That's right . . . I remember reading about her death in the papers — tragic accident. I liked her." He hesitated and then continued, "I guess you need to know since you're handling the file now." He hesitated again. "Mind you, it's only hearsay, I can't prove it, but I'd bet my bank account on it."

"On what?" She glanced at the file in her lap, then looked fixedly at him. "What do I need to know?"

"I think they were lovers." He waited for Randall's reaction. She didn't react.

"I pieced it together. Klein handled all business matters. McKenzie just signed papers." He was still watching for a reaction. "A friend of mine used to work with the firm that did their wills. They have a couple of gay attorneys who attract that kind of business. Klein left everything to McKenzie, and McKenzie left everything to Klein."

Randall's mind was asking more questions. "Klein was fifteen years older than McKenzie."

"Dr. Klein once told me that they met when McKenzie was a medical student. Klein was one of her professors." He leaned forward. "Other than the fact that both women have a good reputation as heart surgeons, that's all I know." He shook his head. "I really am sorry about Dr. Klein. I liked her."

Randall stood. "Thanks for the information." Her hand was on the door knob when Jordan asked, "Does McKenzie's sexual preference present a problem for you in working with her?"

Randall answered without turning around. "Not really, I was just curious." She closed the door behind her.

Chapter 3

Randall arrived one minute early for her appointment and at exactly 5:30 was shown into Megan's office.

"The doctor will be right in," the young receptionist told Randall. "Have a seat."

Randall sat in a wing-back chair and scanned the office. It was spacious. A comfortable looking sofa took up a large portion of one wall; an antique rosewood desk in front of two large windows held a casting of a sculpture on its left-hand corner. Randall recognized the entwined lovers as Rodin's "Eternal Idol."

A striking oil painting of a stormy sea hung on the wall across from the sofa, its shades of gray promising a storm of great intensity. Randall walked to the painting. A neat signature in the lower right-hand corner read "Ellen Klein." A section of the wall held several black and white photographs, one showing two women on skis, the taller of the two with her arm around the shoulders of the other. They looked happy, and somehow warm against a mountain of snow.

Randall moved closer to the photo. Both women were attractive. The shorter one looked younger, but not by fifteen years. Her shoulder-length hair was very dark and very straight. Her eyes were arresting; even in the photograph they contained an energy that looked into people rather than at them, that caught people and held them, if only for an instant. Randall tried to remember where she had seen eyes like that before. Some movie star popular in the forties . . .

The sound of a door opening tore Randall from reverie. She turned to see the eyes in the photograph looking directly at her.

"Hi, I'm Megan McKenzie." Megan extended a hand. "I'm sorry to keep you waiting."

Randall shook Megan's hand and moved again to the wing-back chair. "That's quite all right. I've been looking around. You have an interesting collection. That painting is very good." Randall gestured toward Ellen's seascape.

"Thank you. It's always been one of my favorites. I put it in my office so I'd get to see it more." Megan seated herself behind her desk.

For a moment Megan was captivated by Randall's physical beauty, the delicate features that were enhanced by flawless skin with a natural glow. Her eyes were a light, liquid blue, her hair a radiant auburn. She seemed tall even when seated.

"Do you paint?" Randall asked.

"No. I'm afraid the best I can offer the world of art is appreciation."

"Have you anything else that Dr. Klein has done?"

"Yes, I have quite a few of Ellen's paintings at home." Megan looked at the seascape. "Painting was almost a

13

necessity for her." She forced herself back to the present. "You have some papers that need my attention?"

"Yes, we have several issues to consider." Randall took a thick file from her attache case. "May I use your desk?"

"Please do." Megan cleared aside several files.

Randall pulled her chair to the desk and spread papers out in front of Megan. She was slightly aware of Megan's cologne; it had the fresh, clean scent of vanilla.

"These land leases are up for renewal. I think we can increase the lease price by at least one-third. Any questions?"

Megan looked at papers that might as well have been written in Greek. Ellen had set up the original deals, and that was good enough for her approval.

"I have no questions. If you can get an increase, that's great. What do you think the chances are?"

Randall looked at Megan in disbelief. Not only did Megan not understand her investments, she had not an iota of business sense.

"Your chances for a one-third increase are excellent. The stores leasing the property will not want the inconvenience of relocating." Randall laid out other papers. "This is an offer for two parcels of undeveloped land you own in Gwinnett County. A developer wants to build cluster homes on the land." She waited a second and continued, "I'm sure this is an excellent price. Top dollar." She watched Megan's face for a reaction. Megan's eyes slid across the papers without taking in what was written on them.

"Sounds like a good deal. Do I need to sign somewhere?"

"Not yet. I need to have the contracts drawn up. I should have them in a couple of days." Randall began placing more papers on the desk.

"Look, I don't mean to be difficult, but I really don't understand a lot of this." Megan studied Randall's face. "I'm afraid I'll have to depend on you to point me in the right

14

direction. You seem quite capable, and I'm sure Ellen never would have chosen your firm if she wasn't sure it could handle these things very well."

"Of course we'll handle things, but you still need to know what's being done on your behalf," Randall stated.

Megan smiled and shook her head. "I'm afraid you're dealing with a hopeless case when it comes to business." She gestured at the papers. "I can't take any credit for these investments, and I don't even know what most of them are. I'd like to count on you to handle them from now on. Just keep me posted every now and then, and let me know when you need me to sign something."

Randall's face was a picture of disbelief. Megan laughed. "I'm not crazy, Ms. Grayson. I'm sane enough to know what I don't know. I'm also used to making quick decisions, and I have come to the conclusion that you know real estate very well." Megan smiled. "I trust you. I'm in your hands."

Randall had not expected a business genius, but neither had she expected a complete neophyte. How could a woman bright enough to do open heart surgery be so ignorant about her own best interest in money matters? Randall fought back her annoyance. She began to gather up the papers.

"As you wish. I'll get the contracts ready and get back with you. You'll have to meet with me again in order to iron out any last-minute details and sign the papers." Randall's annoyance slipped out. "Can you manage that?"

Megan laughed. "Your reaction reminds me of Ellen when she first started talking to me about investments. It was at least a year before she accepted the fact that she would have to take care of such things herself. I didn't mean to offend you. I'm just not good at leases and contracts. Can't we just have an agreement? I'll listen attentively to your best advice, and then I'll follow it."

Randall laughed. It was impossible not to like this woman. She extended a hand and shook Megan's. "You have a deal, Doctor. Just be available when I need your okay or your signature."

Megan traced an X over her heart. "Scout's honor. I will be available whenever."

Randall closed her attache case. She looked at Megan. "I'm sorry about Dr. Klein. I've heard such nice things about her. I know it's a terrible loss for you. Good friends are not easy to find."

"Thank you," Megan said simply.

"I really would like to see her paintings some time," Randall said as she moved toward the door.

"I'm afraid I'm not home much," Megan said. She looked at Randall with renewed pleasure in her beauty. "But perhaps we can arrange a time in the future. Remind me and we'll set a date."

Chapter 4

Randall was completing a sales agreement when Kenneth arrived home from his latest business trip. He was a senior partner in the firm, and he was a consultant for a lot of out-of-state cases. He had been gone two weeks on this trip, a week in San Diego, another in San Francisco. In their three years of marriage Kenneth and Randall had spent almost as much time apart as they had together.

They had bought their house three weeks before their wedding. A two-story contemporary with the appearance of a chalet from outside, inside it was an open and spacious house. Aside from the kitchen, two large rooms occupied the entire first floor — a formal dining room and a living room with large windows that overlooked a wooded area. The upper floor was broken up into medium-sized rooms, each cut off from the other, each seeming cold and formal to Randall. She did not like the house.

Climbing the stairs, Kenneth called to Randall. "Where are you?"

"In here," Randall replied from her study.

Kenneth walked in and kissed Randall on the cheek. "How's my favorite lady attorney?"

Randall completed the sentence she was speaking into her dictating machine, and clicked it off. She kissed in her husband's direction. "Just fine. How was your trip? Did the case go well?"

Kenneth sat down on an overstuffed chair. "Not bad. The case was interesting. We won, of course."

"Of course."

"I'll tell you about it over dinner," Kenneth said. "I'm starved. The food on the plane was worse than usual."

Randall laid the dictating machine on her desk and looked at her husband. Forty-eight years old, with silver-gray hair and pale blue eyes, broad-shouldered, and six feet, three inches tall, he would be considered handsome by most women's standards. But, she reflected, his romantic appearance was utterly deceiving. The man was analytical to the core. His mind worked in precise logical steps, and he could be counted on to add an air of stability to any and all situations, even candlelight and music.

Yet she had admired that mind of his from the moment she had met him. As a young attorney, she was impressed by a senior partner who looked like a movie star and thought like Clarence Darrow. Even when she realized that Kenneth was ninety-nine percent computer, she was still attracted to him, holding a secret hope that beneath the logical mind beat the heart of a secret but true romantic. For the first nine months of their marriage Randall had prepared candlelight dinners and rented romantic old movies in an attempt to break through to that vein she hoped to either find or create in him. Finally she put away the candles and started bringing home the westerns and detective stories that Kenneth loved. After all, she consoled herself, romance wasn't the most important part of a good marriage. Consistency and stability counted for an awful lot. Her life did become more and more consistent; one day followed the other like identical twins. Her work was now the only area of her life that held the promise of the unexpected and the exciting.

"I'll fix something for you," she said.

"Are you almost finished with what you're doing?" Kenneth asked.

"I'll come back to it later. I probably have a couple more hours on it."

Kenneth got up. "You work on that. I'll fix myself something. I'd like you to come upstairs early tonight. I'd like to have sex, and I have an early appointment in the morning."

There was a time when Randall would have been offended by such a matter-of-fact approach, but this was Kenneth's way, and she had grown used to it.

"I should be ready about ten." She picked up the dictating equipment, clicked it on, and began dictating.

Chapter 5

Randall was half way through a glass of club soda when the hostess showed Megan to the booth. Megan had kept the promise of availability she had made earlier, and Randall had set up a dinner meeting at Chequers.

"Would you like a drink? A glass of wine?" Randall asked.

"Just ginger ale, thanks. I don't drink during the week," Megan replied.

"Thanks for coming." Randall smiled. "This is much nicer than meeting in your office."

The restaurant was one of the few in Atlanta with booths as well as tables for two. The rich woods and translucent glass partitions added both atmosphere and privacy — a perfect blend of elegance and causal warmth.

The two women talked amicably about books, movies, and restaurants until the waiter served after-dinner coffee.

"Dr. McKenzie," Randall began.

"Megan," Megan said.

"Megan." Randall smiled. "I'm not sure exactly how to say what I'm about to, so please hear me out before you respond."

Megan's eyes fastened on Randall. She felt herself stiffen slightly.

Randall looked directly into Megan's pale grey eyes and saw pain and caution gazing back. "You and I will be working together on a fairly regular basis. I'd like us to be honest with each other. I've met you exactly twice, counting tonight, and I like you very much. I don't want to have to guard my words with you."

Randall took a small swallow of coffee. "To put it bluntly, I've been told that you and Dr. Klein were more than business partners. I have been told that you and she were lovers."

Randall paused briefly, but Megan gave no sign of response.

"I want you to know that I couldn't care less what your sexual orientation is. Whatever it is, is none of my business. The only reason I mention the subject at all is that I don't want to be forced to carefully avoid it. Also, the loss of a mate can be a devastating experience and can affect one's judgments."

Randall's voice became even softer. "You ignored three letters and several phone calls before I finally convinced you to see me. It's obvious that something major has happened in your life. I think that major event was the death of your lover, and I want you to know that you can be honest with me about it. We have an attorney-client relationship; anything you say to me is confidential."

Randall smiled and leaned forward just a little. "I'm not raising this issue with you because I'm nosey or curious. I'm raising it because I'm responsible for a large amount of your money, and when I ask how you feel about this investment or that, I have to know some of what's going on in your head in order to give you the best possible advice."

Randall took a deep breath. "So there. I've said my piece. What are you thinking?"

Megan was slightly stunned. She had not expected such point-blank confrontation, but there it was. Randall had made a fairly good case for her need to know.

"I'm not used to discussing my personal life with people I hardly know. However, you do make a good case." Megan sipped her coffee. "As your client, and claiming that privilege, I admit that Ellen and I were lovers. Whoever gave you the information guessed correctly. I just hope they didn't embroider the story too much."

"There were no details," Randall assured her. "I was curious as to why an intelligent woman cared so little about more than a million dollars' worth of investments. I asked one of the firm's attorneys what he knew about you two, and he said he thought you were lovers. It made more sense to me then, since I could understand that a person who had just lost her mate might not be interested in investments or anything else for a while. That's all there was to it."

Randall's eyes softened. "I'm sorry, Megan. You two must have really had a great relationship."

Megan heard the sincerity in Randall's voice and was touched by it. "Thanks for your concern." She managed a brief smile. "I must admit I didn't expect this conversation."

The waiter brought more coffee. "I heard that you met Dr. Klein in medical school, " Randall said. She savored a bite of cheesecake.

"That's right."

"I didn't mean to make you uncomfortable," Randall offered.

"You didn't really. It's just that thinking about Ellen hurts." Her face softened and brightened slightly. "We were very much in love. Even after eight years. We had the kind of relationship that only gets better with time." Megan sighed. "I miss her so much."

Randall could see the tears in Megan's eyes. "I wish I had met her; she must have been quite a person."

"She's responsible for my practicing cardiology. She was an absolutely brilliant woman." Megan brushed a tear away with the back of her hand.

"Tell me about her."

"Why?" Was this mere curiosity from a heterosexual woman, idle prying?

"Because I can feel that she was a very special person, because she meant so much to you. And because I'd like to know the kind of woman you were that much in love with." Randall sipped her coffee. "For all of the above and more." She smiled warmly. "Please."

Reassured, Megan leaned back in the booth.

"When we met, Ellen wasn't looking for a romantic involvement with anyone, least of all a student. But something in us clicked. We were more of everything when we were together. I was attracted to her the first day I saw her in class. She needed a research assistant. I was the best and the brightest, so I got the job. We saw each other every day, and we talked a lot.

"We were both in love with medicine, and from that starting point we discovered each other. It was six months as strictly teacher and student before either of us admitted to the other that we were in love."

Megan's eyes softened. For a moment Randall and the present didn't exist. Like a leaf caught in the wind, memories spun Megan through time and again it was the first time.

* * * * *

They lay naked on Ellen's bed. It was summer and the room was sweet with daylight and sunshine. The pale blue sheets were cool and clean against their skin.

Megan felt her body respond as Ellen's lips moved lightly against her own. Soft velvet lips that brushed her cheeks, her forehead, her eyes. Warm lips that parted easily against her open mouth and took Megan's tongue inside.

Gentle hands, soft as silk, moving down Megan's body, kneading and caressing, leaving pleasure in their path. Ellen's hands moving between her thighs, fingers finding the small wet pool and dipping inside. Ellen's hand finding the satin pearl, caressing it with Megan's own wetness.

Megan's mouth pushed firmly against Ellen's as passion and pleasure began their climb inside her. Her hand rested on Ellen's head as Ellen's warm mouth caressed her breasts. Ellen lingered there, holding her nipples gently with her teeth, sucking them into her mouth, massaging them with her tongue. All the while Ellen's fingers continued dipping into the pool, bringing new wetness to the pearl.

Warm softness, Ellen's tongue against her inner thighs, against the satin folds, against the pearl. Pleasure and passion moving through Megan leaving no part of her untouched. Gentle sucking motions pulled her inside. She pushed Ellen's head against herself as she felt the quick, firm strokes of her tongue. A low, murmuring sound spoke Ellen's own excitement, pushing Megan's pleasure higher. Passion moved through Megan, renewing itself as Ellen's strokes grew more rapid, her murmuring louder, their pleasure deeper. Joy upon joy. Unexplored pleasure, a frontier beyond, union. . . .

* * * * *

"Megan," Randall's voice called Megan back to the present, "you left me in mid-story. What happened next? Did you live together right away?"

Megan focused on Randall again. "It was about two months before we moved in together." She tasted the hot coffee the waiter had poured into her cup.

"Ellen was not only witty and caring, she was a gifted teacher and surgeon. She donated a lot of time to the free clinic. Not many people knew about that."

She took another sip of coffee. "But above everything else, she was warm and tender and gave two hundred percent of herself to whatever and whoever she made a commitment to. I was lucky. I was the whoever. And if I live to be five hundred, I will never find anyone like her or love anyone as much."

Megan gestured with her cup. "So there you have it, Counselor, the story — a brief synopsis of the love of my life, the only woman I have ever loved, the only woman I can imagine sharing my life with. Comments?"

"Just two. I hope before I die I will love someone that much and be loved that much in return. You're a very lucky woman."

It was Megan's chance to ask questions: "What about your marriage?"

"It leaves empty places," Randall answered honestly. "It's safe, consistent, stable . . . but it doesn't touch the soul. I'd almost forgotten that a relationship can touch the soul. Listening to you reminds me of the marriage I'd hoped to have. Most of the time I never give a thought to the fact that not every marriage is like mine. I settle for what I have and tell myself it could be worse."

Randall looked at Megan pensively. "Besides, I don't think the kind of relationships you had with Ellen is just waiting out there to be claimed. You two had something rare. You would have been the best of friends, even if you'd not been lovers. I don't know any of my married friends who have the kind of relationship you described. It wouldn't be possible with Kenneth."

"Why do you stay married if you're not happy?" Megan's tone contained bewilderment.

"Because I like the advantages of being married to Kenneth. And because I'm not really unhappy. I haven't seen any of my friends doing any better. Kenneth is basically a good man; he just doesn't feel things deeply. I guess he doesn't feel love deeply either."

"You do make love, don't you?" Megan felt oddly free to ask Randall anything.

Randall pondered the question. "We have sex. I've never given it much thought before, but I don't think Kenneth has ever used the phrase 'make love.'" She was speaking as much to herself as to Megan. "He's a very logical and detached man. I don't remember him expressing passion over anything. He lives on a horizontal line with no peaks or valleys." Randall smiled weakly. "Do you suppose that I've married a robot?"

Megan found it difficult to understand why anyone would stay in the kind of marriage Randall had just described. "Have you considered therapy? I have a friend who's a psychiatrist."

Randall laughed. "Kenneth would be the first to tell you that only unstable people need therapy. He, on the other hand, is so stable it's frightening."

The waiter brought the check, and Randall handed him a credit card. "My treat," she said. "You can fix me take-out gourmet in the microwave sometime."

Megan smiled warmly at Randall. "That's a deal. You wanted to see Ellen's paintings. Would you like to come for dinner next Tuesday?"

"Tuesday would be great."

Megan took a notebook from her purse and sketched a map to her house.

"Before you put that pen away, I need your signature on these papers," Randall reminded her.

Chapter 6

Lynn Bradley threw another log on the fire and poked at the ashes with a foot. Megan watched her,thinking that Lynn's appearance was a blend of distinguished physician and well-conditioned athlete. Her trim body was tall and agile, her light green eyes alive and intelligent, hinting at the keen mind, the constantly involved intellect that moved relentlessly behind them.

Lynn looked around the den, her favorite room in Megan's house. The soft cream carpet and dark brown leather sofa created a genuine feeling of warmth and comfort. A large fieldstone fireplace ran from floor to ceiling and occupied most of one wall, multiplying the room's easiness.

"That's a good way to get burned, Dr. Bradley," Megan said as she handed Lynn a mug of coffee.

"I've been burned before." Lynn arranged the screen in front of the fireplace. "Word has it that the deal on your Gwinnett property went through."

"True." Megan laughed. "Where do you get your information? I sometimes have the feeling that you're treating nine out of every ten people who know me, and they're telling you all the details of my every day life."

"I have spies everywhere." Lynn sipped her coffee. "How much did you get for the land?"

"Precisely one point three million dollars. Do I look like a millionaire?"

"You will to the IRS. How are you investing it?"

"You'd be proud of me. I've been working with that law firm Ellen selected, and they're handling the sales and the reinvestment for me."

"Good. You're behaving well. That mountain of unopened mail cluttering your study — did you open it or burn it?"

"I opened it." Megan smiled. "Actually, the attorney is responsible for that, too." She told Lynn about her meeting and conversation with Randall Grayson, her admission to Randall of the relationship with Ellen.

"Uh-huh!" Lynn smirked.

"Uh-huh, what?" Megan asked, unaccountably annoyed.

"Sounds to me like the curious married kind. 'My husband doesn't understand me; maybe you can.' "

Megan shook her head. "It's nothing like that. The woman is straight. She was just clearing the air for a better business relationship."

"Meggie, you are so naive! The woman is most likely curious about what sex with a woman is like."

"No way. There wasn't the slightest hint of anything like that. The only relationship Randall Grayson is interested in is attorney-client."

"Who's talking relationship? I'm talking married woman seeks cheap thrill."

"Randall is not looking for any action on the side. And believe me, I'm not either," Megan said emphatically. "We're talking real estate here, Lynn, just real estate."

"Let's hope so. You're much too good a catch to be wasted on a wanton woman." Lynn smiled. "Besides, if you want a little action, I make house calls."

"Thank you, Doctor." Megan threw a sofa pillow at her. "If I feel an uncontrollable urge, you'll be the first person I'll call."

Lynn's voice took on a serious tone. "You know, I could fall in love with you with very little provocation." Lynn knew she was compromising the truth. She was already in love with Megan.

"You have my word. If I feel an uncontrollable urge, I'll bring my business to you." Megan smiled. "You're my dearest friend, but I'm not in love with you."

Lynn could see that Megan had taken none of her words seriously. She grinned, deciding to let go of the subject lightly. "Not yet, you're not, but who knows what tomorrow will bring?"

"Is that why you want to go to Aspen with me? To wear me down?"

Lynn's grin grew even wider. "You can use the four-day weekend and so can I. What better place than your lodge in Aspen?" She raised an eyebrow. "Now if you happen to be hit by an uncontrollable urge to do something besides ski —"

Megan laughed at her. How dear of Lynn to try to deflect her grief into more healthy channels. "You're the nicest and craziest psychiatrist I know." She took Lynn's hand. "I do need you, Lynn. You're my closest friend."

Lynn was aware of the warmth of Megan's hand. For what must have been the thousandth time, she fought the desire to kiss her. Lynn smiled. "You missed your calling. You should have been a psychiatrist — or a diplomat."

Chapter 7

"I certainly like your home," Randall told Megan as they walked into the den.

She had had no trouble locating the house. It was set solidly atop a cliff overlooking the Chattahoochee River, andneatly trimmed ivy covered much of it's English Tudor facade. The den lay at the end of the entrance hall. The twenty by thirty foot room was dominated by a massive stone fireplace and rosewood bookcases. A large oil painting above the fireplace depicted a river, white with rapids and banked on each side by tall Canadian hemlocks. A gray sky threatened a storm that was already bending the trees in its path. Like the seascape in Megan's office, the painting also suggested unlimited energy.

Megan gave her a tour of the house. Ellen's paintings decorated every room. Afterward Randall stood before the fireplace looking at the painting of the river. "Now that I've seen Ellen's other work, I can see that this one captures the heart of her gift. It has the same feeling as the seascape on your office wall."

Megan had poured two cups of amaretto coffee, and she handed one of the pottery mugs to Randall.

"It's my second favorite." Megan eased into a chair and gazed at the painting. "Ellen was one of the few who could have made a living as an artist if she'd chosen to."

"Have you ever considered showing the paintings? There must be twenty of them."

"Twenty-three in this house." Megan's eyes had not moved from the painting. "I don't want to show them. I like having them here for myself." She looked at Randall. "To be shared with a select few."

"I'm complimented."

"Actually, you're the only person who has asked specifically to see them. Ellen would have been delighted."

"I have the feeling that I'm one of the select few to be invited into your home."

"There've been a few cocktail parties, a few formal dinners. No more than necessary. I don't really like entertaining, and I enjoy time to myself." She smiled, admiring Randall's trim figure, taking note of the camel pants and soft brown sweater that showed off Randall's auburn hair. "You would have liked Ellen. She was much more gregarious than I."

"I like you," Randall said casually. "I get more than my fill of cocktail parties and chit-chat during the week. I sometimes wonder if the other people at the parties are as bored as I am." She sipped her coffee. "But in my line of work I have to defer to clients or they'll take their business elsewhere."

"Are you always as blunt with them as you were with me the other night? I could have told you to mind your own business and taken my investments elsewhere. You took a big chance."

"Somehow I was sure you wouldn't do that. I figured you'd either tell me I should mind my own business or you'd just plain deny any relationship other than friendship with Dr. Klein. I didn't see you as the type to take your business elsewhere as a punishment for honesty and frankness. I guess I could have been wrong, but I'm glad I wasn't."

"Let me give you some advice." Megan poured more coffee. "Don't try that on anyone else. You might do worse than just lose their business."

Randall sat down and put her mug on the end table. "I did offend you then. I'm really sorry."

"I wasn't really offended. Shocked a little. Curious as to why you wanted to know. But not offended." Megan smiled. "A lot of people do business with gay people every day, but they usually don't actually come out and ask for confirmation of their suspicions."

Randall leaned back in her chair. "I see your point. All I can tell you is, when I'm curious I usually try to satisfy that curiosity. I was curious about you so I asked."

The doorbell rang. Lynn Bradley looked distracted when Megan opened the beveled glass door.

"Just thought I'd stop by and give you the bad news in person. I can't go with you to Aspen next weekend."

Lynn stopped short when she saw Randall. "I'm sorry, I didn't realize you had company."

Megan made the introductions. Randall extended a hand and Lynn took it.

"Please, don't let me intrude," Lynn said. Turning back to Megan, she added, "I wanted to let you know about next

34

weekend. Jim Colby just had an emergency appendectomy, I have to cover for him."

"Sit down, Lynn. I'll get you some coffee —"

"No, thanks. I really can't stay. I'm very tired — two emergencies tonight. Sorry about next weekend, Megan. You should go anyway, though. You could use the break."

"I'll think about it," Megan said as she walked Lynn to the door.

Lynn whispered, "You're not getting involved with your attorney, are you?"

"Don't be ridiculous," Megan said emphatically. "I have no interest whatever in Randall Grayson."

"You may not be interested in her, but I'm betting the lady is interested in you. That's my professional judgment."

"It wouldn't matter if she were. I told you, I'm not ready for a new relationship, and I'm not interested in a one-night stand." Megan felt mildly annoyed.

Lynn leaned forward and kissed Megan on the cheek. "Watch yourself, Meggie. Curious women can be dangerous." Lynn smiled broadly. "And so can their husbands."

"Get out of here," Megan sputtered. "Go home and get some sleep. I'll talk to you tomorrow."

Megan returned to the den and found Randall adding a log to the fire. "I hope you don't mind," Randall said. "I love fireplaces."

Megan sat down and took a sip of her coffee. "I have a fire almost every night," she said. "Tell me a little about what you enjoy doing — other than practicing law and making money."

"I'm on the board of the art museum. And I like to ski. In fact, now that your friend can't go with you, do you need a companion on that Aspen weekend? Kenneth is involved in a big case in Chicago and I could use a long weekend myself."

Megan hesitated.

"If I'm intruding," Randall said quickly, "if you were planning to ask someone else to go with you, please just be honest with me."

"It's not that. I'm just not the life of the party on ski trips. I like to spend time by myself. If you don't mind that, you're welcome to come along."

Randall smiled. "I don't mind that one bit. I'm pretty much of a loner myself. You can see me when we leave for Aspen and when we come back, if that's what you'd like."

Megan laughed. "I'm not quite that bad, Randall. I don't hate people. I just don't want you to expect to be entertained." Megan smiled warmly. "If a great place to ski and beautiful country really appeals to you, you're more than welcome to come along. In fact, I'd enjoy the company."

"Great!" Randall's eyes showed her excitement. "When do we leave? Do you want me to make reservations with any particular airline?"

"I'll have my receptionist change Lynn's reservations to your name. We leave about eleven next Thursday morning, we'll get back about five-thirty on Monday. We'll be staying at my lodge. Can you fit that into your schedule?"

"Sounds terrific. I'll call in the morning and give your receptionist a credit card number." Randall stood and moved to stand in front of the fire. She looked around the den. "I really like this room. It's very comfortable. I'm glad you invited me."

Megan looked at her with pleasure, anticipating several days in the company of this intelligent, interesting woman. "I am too."

Chapter 8

No matter how often Megan visited Aspen she was charmed by the contrast between quaint village and the overpowering landscape. She parked the rented car outside the town, and she and Randall took one of the free shuttle buses into the village of picturesque Victorian buildings nestled on the side of Aspen Mountain — Ajax to the skiers who traveled its slopes. The town was crowded with people who were bundled up in ski clothes and in a holiday mood.

"This is marvelous," Randall said. "It's like stepping back in time. I don't know why I've never skied here before."

Megan was pleased to be the one to introduce Randall to Aspen's spectacular beauty.

They window shopped for an hour before catching a shuttle bus back to the car. They stocked up on staples and gourmet treats and headed for the lodge.

"How far is it from town?" Randall asked as they began the climb out of the valley.

"About four miles." Megan kept her eyes on the road. "I called the caretaker last week, so it should be aired out and clean. A lot of dust and cobwebs can gather in a year."

"Did you use the place much before Ellen's death?"

"About every three weeks for a long weekend. Both of us loved to ski. We liked the stillness and solitude of the place even more. Ellen bought the lodge years before I met her. It would be impossible to duplicate here today for what she paid."

"I know what you mean. Land here is about as cheap as downtown Manhattan."

They pulled off the main road and headed up the mountain.

"It's so very beautiful," Randall said as she took in the snow-covered slopes covered with trees. "I love snow."

"That gray sky looks like more of it," Megan said as she pulled the car onto a narrow paved road that seemed to climb straight up the mountain. "When we get around this curve, you can see the lodge. It's no castle, but it serves its purpose."

A sturdy looking two-story structure of field stone and cedar, the lodge seemed to Randall to grow out of the mountainside. She walked into the great room on the first floor which served as living room, dining room, and den. The walls were tongue-and-groove cedar; large cedar beams crossed the ceiling. Furniture arranged in groups broke the room into cozy conversation areas. Black leather loveseats faced each other in front of a large stone fireplace; a black Alpaca rug covered a large area of the hardwood floor from the loveseats to the edge of the stone hearth. Sunlight made its way through four large windows and added warmth even without a fire.

"Nice," Randall said.

"Let me show you to your room," Megan offered.

They climbed the stairs to a long hallway. Megan pointed to the room closest to the landing.

Randall walked into a large room with hardwood floors and a rust-colored area rug, in its center a queen-size bed with a bright quilt. An antique dresser and chest of drawers were to one side, a comfortable looking recliner faced two large windows.

Randall walked to the window. "I can't even see another house."

"The closest one is about a quarter mile from here," Megan said. "Get changed and we'll head for Ajax. We can get in a few hours of skiing before dinner."

She walked slowly from the room, feeling that Randall's presence did not fill the emptiness left in the house by Ellen's death.

The ski lift was only ten minutes from the lodge. They bought a five-day lift ticket — they could choose from any of the seven lifts which climbed Ajax.

The air was clean and crisp as they began their lift ride up the mountain. There had been several good snowfalls, and the mountain had a solid base with five or six inches of powder on its runs. As they rode the lift, Megan thought about the many times she and Ellen had made the same trip. Her mind was filled with Ellen's face, red-cheeked and bright, smiling at her through the falling snow. She heard Ellen's voice and the sound of her laughter as she challenged Megan to a race down the mountain.

"If I win," Ellen would always say, "you take me to dinner every night we're here. If you win, you get to decide whether I cook at home or take you out."

Megan smiled as she remembered how Ellen always won. Megan let go of the memories in time to exit the ski lift gracefully. She automatically moved toward what she knew was the fastest run.

"Race you to the bottom," Randall challenged.

Megan hesitated.

"Come on," Randall said. "After all, you have the advantage. You know the run and I don't."

"You're on," Megan declared.

As both skiers cleared the crest of the run, Randall called to Megan: "Loser buys dinner!"

Megan could hear Randall's laughter as she pulled ahead and increased her speed. She called to Megan over her shoulder, "Come on, Doc, you can move faster than that. My grandmother could beat you."

Megan accepted the challenge, and the race was on. They exchanged the lead several times, but Randall reached the bottom first. She turned quickly and her smile was as wide as a child's. "You owe me dinner!"

Megan felt exhilarated. "You only beat me by three ski-lengths!"

"No quibbling, Doctor. A cat's whisker is as good as a mile." She moved closer to Megan and looked directly into her eyes. Her voice became very solemn. "As they say in the legal profession, 'You lose, you pay!' " Randall's face broke into a wide grin.

Megan shook her head and laughed. "I wish I could tell you what a pleasure it is to lose to such a gracious winner."

"Touche! Now, where are you taking me for dinner?"

Megan bought dinner at Louigi's, a small Italian restaurant on the outskirts of Aspen. When they returned to the lodge, Megan built a fire.

Before long both women, having changed into jogging pants and sweat shirts, were settled comfortably opposite each other on the two loveseats and were watching the fire.

Randall took a sip of her coffee. "You'll either have to learn to ski faster or get used to buying dinner."

"You think so?" Megan chuckled.

"Most definitely. Let's have a standard bet. One race at the end of the day to determine where you'll buy dinner that night."

"Where *I'll* buy dinner?" Megan feigned outrage. "Be careful, arrogance is very easy to stumble over."

Randall smiled. "You've mistaken my humility for arrogance."

"You have humility?" Megan asked mischievously. "It would take a microscope to find it."

"Not so," Randall replied. "The nuns taught me that humility is truth, and since I'm simply being truthful, I'm also being humble."

"So you blame your big head on the nuns?" Megan was enjoying their sparring. "What would the sisters say if they knew you were taking advantage of their spiritual advice to feed your stomach instead of your soul?"

"Not much. They were already disappointed in me when I didn't enter the convent after high school. Not that I ever wanted to — I didn't. But Sister Mary Paul had religious hopes for me. She almost cried when I told her I wanted to be an attorney."

Randall adjusted the pillow she was leaning against. Her face became serious. "I guess I'm not much of a Catholic any more. I haven't been to Mass in six years. I just can't believe everything they teach. As I get older, truth becomes a lot more complicated."

"You sound sad about that," Megan commented. "Maybe you're being too hard on yourself. I'm no theologian, but it seems to me that spiritual beliefs are more important than religious rituals. In my opinion, a person doesn't have to be religious in order to be good, but one does need spiritual values in order to be truly good."

"What do you define as spiritual beliefs and values?" Randall's voice contained genuine interest. "What do you think makes a person good?"

"Well, take Ellen for instance. She believed in God. She believed in the existence of a soul that survives death. She also believed in the inherent value of all living creatures. She was kind, she went out of her way to help people, she never took advantage of people who were not as bright as she, or as influential as she. She practiced in her everyday life the things that most people just give lip service to." Megan smiled. "Like Ellen, these spiritual values are important to me, too. More important than attending Mass or a prayer meeting."

She paused to look for a moment into Randall's intent face. "Ellen accepted her own humanity, her own limitations. As a doctor, she knew she could administer medicine but she couldn't make it take effect. That's a humbling realization. I think most physicians, consciously or unconsciously, fight for the upper hand over death. But Ellen knew she was not all powerful, and with that knowledge she accepted people without judging them for not living up to her standards. She truly cared about people — warts and all. I asked her one day if she thought prayer helped people. She told me that what a person does with his or her life is the only prayer that really matters." Megan sipped her coffee. "I've come to agree with her."

Randall saw the energy and intensity she had seen for the first time in the photograph in Megan's office. She sat very still. For a moment she was conscious of her breathing. "I think I can understand why you and Ellen loved each other." Her voice was very soft. "You were both very lucky people."

Megan smiled. "This very lucky person is getting very sleepy. If I'm to have any chance of having you buy my dinner tomorrow, I need to get to bed."

Chapter 9

Megan and Randall spent Friday skiing. Megan lost the race by a wider margin, and Randall again selected Louigi's for her second victory dinner.

"Losing to you could become very expensive," Megan said as they returned home after dinner.

"Is that a plea for mercy?"

"Just my pride shedding a few tears. I need something I can beat you at. Do you play chess?"

"Almost as well as I ski," Randall answered with a cocky grin.

"We'll see about that. Let's play a game. The loser buys dinner tomorrow night." Megan was already heading for the chess set on a shelf by the fireplace.

As the two women played in concentrated silence, the fire sent intermittent showers of sparks into the air, a few escaping the screen, hurling themselves into the room, disappearing before they reached the rug.

The game lasted exactly twenty minutes. Megan wore her child's grin as she looked at Randall across the board.

Shrugging, Randall raised her hands in surrender. "Why do I feel that I was set up by the Minnesota Fats of the chess world? Did you work your way through medical school by demolishing students and faculty on the chess board?"

"Would I set you up?" Megan deadpanned.

"You bet!"

"Actually, I have played in a few tournaments." Megan's eyes sparkled with mischief. "In this country and in Europe."

Randall laughed. "You competitive bitch!"

"Guilty, as charged, Counselor. I told you I needed something I could beat you at." Megan leaned back in her chair and said smugly, "You buy dinner tomorrow."

Randall warmed their coffee. "Despite the fact that you took shameful advantage of me, I'll pay my debt. However, I'll pay my debt on my terms. I'll buy dinner but cook it here."

"You can cook?"

"You should be ashamed of yourself for asking that question — you, the microwave queen of Georgia. It just so happens that I'm a very good cook. I don't do it very often, but I do it very well. And no more bets over chess — unless I'm in the mood to lose. And I always play to win."

"I have a day to think of something else," Megan said, moving to the fireplace. "Would you like some music?"

"Yes," Randall said as she settled on the floor with her back resting against a loveseat. "The fire feels good. I love the sound of the wood popping."

"Me, too." Megan started the cassette deck and sat on the rug opposite Randall as the sounds of a violin floated into the room.

"Isaac Stern?" Randall asked.

Megan nodded. "I love violin music. It touches every corner of my soul."

They listened in silence, watching sparks break free of the logs and dance briefly before they disappeared. Randall was aware of the light from the fire as it moved on Megan's face. She could see the flames reflected in Megan's light gray eyes, tiny flames that seemed to belong there. She felt drawn to those flames, aware that she wanted to touch the light as it touched Megan. Her hand was resting on the smooth Alpaca rug, and she moved her fingers into and through its softness.

"How did you know you were gay?" Randall suddenly asked.

Megan turned and looked at Randall. Her eyes were warm, and Randall could see the flames dancing up and down within them.

"I was always attracted to women." Megan spoke softly. "When other girls my age were getting crushes on boys, I was getting crushes on the other girls. I wanted to be with them, I wanted them to like me best, to want to spend time with me. As I got older and the crushes matured, I found myself wanting to touch Deborah Phillips. We were both sixteen. I would sit for hours fighting the desire to touch her face with my fingertips."

Randall watched Megan's eyes. "And did you touch her?"

Megan smiled. "No, but I can still remember what it was like to want to so badly. I touched her face a hundred times in my mind but never in reality."

Randall brushed fingertips over her own face, her lips. She knew now that she wanted to touch Megan's face. She fought

46

to control the desire and to diminish the anxiety it provoked within her.

"Was Deborah gay, too?" Randall asked.

"I don't know. Nothing ever happened. Deborah's father got a promotion, and she and her family moved to Texas. I never saw her again. As far as I know, she never knew I had a crush on her."

"It must have been difficult to hide something you felt so strongly."

"It still is," Megan said pensively, moving a slim hand through her hair. "Being gay in a straight world is a lot more complicated than most people ever consider."

"It can't be much more complicated than going through the motions of a marriage where there's no genuine feeling," Randall said softly.

"There's no comparison," Megan said with a touch of sharpness. "Even in a loveless marriage you have society's approval. You can introduce yourself as a couple. But if you're gay, you can't just announce your love to family and friends. In fact, you'll more than likely spend a lot of time denying that you have any such feelings at all. If your family or straight friends find out, chances are they'll disown or at least reject you. If your partner gets sick, you can't call work and say, 'My lover has the flu and I need to stay home and take care of her.' You'll never be quite sure which friends would still be friends if they knew about you. People you've known all your life can suddenly act as if they don't know you at all when they find out you're in love with a woman. It often makes little difference to them that two gay people are committed to each other and have been for five, ten, twenty or more years. They'll more readily accept a straight person, even if that person goes from one one-night stand to another."

Gazing down at the carpet, Megan continued bitterly, "Churches would just as soon hang a bell around the neck of each gay person just as they did with lepers in biblical times. Most gay people lead a double life. They have to in order to survive."

"Not all gays lead a double life," Randall interjected softly. "A lot of them are out and fighting the system. What do you think of their openness?"

"I admire it. It takes real, raw courage." Megan took a swallow of her coffee. "It also takes more than one kind of soldier to win a war. People like me are fighting too. I give my time and my money to support gay rights groups. It takes a lot of both commodities to get laws changed. You're an attorney, you know what it costs to bring a case before the court, what it costs to appeal a loss through all the necessary courts before it can ever reach the Supreme Court."

Megan's eyes grew more intent. "But without the people who are out there on the front lines changing attitudes, nothing would ever begin to get done. They put it all on the line. They're like the civil rights marchers of the Sixties."

"Did you ever think of living more openly as a gay woman?"

"It's crossed my mind. I speak up when someone makes a joke or a snide remark about gays in my presence. I work with Fourth Tuesday, a group of lesbians in the professional community, and with AIDS Atlanta. I buy all my books at Charis in Five Points — it's our feminist bookstore. I have the ear of several legislators, I exert my influence in favor of gay rights whenever I can. Unfortunately, if they knew I was gay, they wouldn't listen to me the way they do now."

Megan took another swallow from her mug. "I may be behind the scenes, but I'm not out of touch with my sisters and brothers. A lot of gay people I know are in their late thirties or older and they live completely in the closet. I feel sorry for them. They're cheating themselves out of their own community. Some of them don't even know another gay person — except their lover. And when something happens to one of them, the other is devastated and left without a support group who can really understand what they're feeling. I think they're more to be understood and pitied than criticized. I couldn't live like they do. I'm not in the front lines, but I'm far from closeted. Most of my real friends, the people who know and accept me as I am, are gay. For gay people, friends become family."

"Not everyone heterosexual is that narrow-minded." Randall said defensively. "I don't condemn gay people."

Megan smiled. "No. But you're not the run-of-the-mill Jane Doe."

"Well, thank you. I thought you'd never notice."

"I've noticed," Megan teased. "All kidding aside, I do like you — very much. You're bright, witty, easy to talk to. God knows you ask more questions than a quiz show, but I'm beginning to accept that as part of your unique charm."

Randall felt great warmth toward Megan. She wanted more than ever to reach to her, to say with a touch, I care about you. I hold you dear. I feel a tenderness toward you that only a gentle touch can speak.

Randall suddenly realized that Megan was standing. "I'm sorry to call an end to a very nice evening," Megan said, "but I'm afraid I'm about to fall asleep."

"Me too," Randall said. "See you bright and early."

Megan turned at the top of the stairs and smiled into Randall's eyes. "Sleep warm, Randall."

Chapter 10

Snow during the night had laid a clean white blanket under a beautiful day. Only the flat tracks of skiers and the tiny footprints of fur-covered creatures seeking out an early breakfast were visible. The snow crunched under Megan's and Randall's boots as they carried their skis to the lift area which was wonderfully uncrowded, like quiet city streets on an early Sunday morning.

They were among the first to exit the ski lift and make their way down the mountain. Megan selected a different run this time, one that lent itself to short fast runs and periods of cross-country skiing. They talked and laughed during the cross-country and shared each other's enthusiasm for the downhill sections.

They took a quick break to sip steamy cups of hot chocolate, then talked about which run to try next.

"Why not the run we just finished?" Randall suggested. She didn't mention the reason — that she had enjoyed the slower stretches where they had been able to talk.

Halfway down the mountain, exhilarated by the sheer beauty around her, Randall started a snowball fight. Megan kicked her skis loose and ran over to wash Randall's face with snow. Randall released her own skis and grabbed Megan, wrestling her to the ground, throwing her body across Megan. She rubbed a large handful of snow into Megan's face. "Wait a minute! Time out!" Megan pleaded through her hysterical laughter. "I can't see. There's snow inside my goggles!"

Randall stopped but did not take her body from Megan's. "No tricks," she threatened. "You have a truce only to clear your vision."

"Honest, no tricks." Megan pushed her goggles back on her forehead and brushed the snow away from her eyes and face. "Are you going to keep me pinned here forever?" Megan asked, laughing up at Randall.

As she looked into Megan's eyes, Randall felt her heartbeat quicken. Her face was only inches from Megan's, she could feel Megan's body heat.

Suddenly her eyes locked with Megan's, and all the laughter stopped. Randall felt a strong desire to lean forward, to touch Megan's lips with her own. Her hands were shaking slightly, she had an undefinable sensation in the pit of her stomach.

Megan reached to Randall's face. "You have snow all over your own goggles." Lightly she brushed the snow away. "Can you see better now?" Megan asked, not breaking their locked gaze.

Randall didn't answer; she was mesmerized by the pale gray energy in Megan's eyes.

51

"Randall," Megan said softly, "you'd better let me up before we freeze."

Randall pulled her goggles down over her eyes, hoping to hide her chaotic feelings behind their dark tint. "Okay," she said lightly. "You can get up, but remember I won the snowball fight."

Megan laughed and Randall could feel the danger move away. Not far away, but far enough so that she did not have to own the danger she still felt.

Chapter 11

Dinner included veal marsala with fresh mushrooms and a side dish of linguine with a delicate tomato sauce. "After so perfect a dinner," Megan said with a sigh of contentment, "how about Isaac Stern again? Some Rubenstein, and some more wine?"

Again they settled on the rug in front of the fireplace, this time comfortably silent. Again Randall watched the light from the fire dance on Megan's face. Moonlight streamed through the large windows and made its own patterns on the floor and walls. Music mixed with wine and warmth, and again Randall felt pulled to Megan. She thought of Megan's eyes gazing up at her from the snow and again she felt a strong desire to reach to her, to touch her gently. As she remembered Megan lightly brushing the snow from her face, she felt her breathing quicken. She wanted to feel Megan's hand again.

"Megan." Randall's voice seemed to blend with the music.

Megan turned to face Randall. Again Randall could see the tiny flames as they danced in Megan's eyes.

"When you mentioned Deborah last night," Randall said carefully, "you said one of the ways you knew you were gay was that you wanted to touch her. Just because a woman wants to touch another woman doesn't make her gay, does it?" Randall could hear the anxiety in her own voice.

"It was the way I felt about touching her," Megan said in an objective tone. "The way I wanted to touch her. I knew that my touch, if it was unwelcomed, could end our friendship." She took a swallow of wine. "I wanted to express tenderness toward her. It was my motivation that made it different. How many of your female friends have *you* ever wanted to touch like that?"

Panic surged through Randall. That undefinable sensation was back in the pit of her stomach. Her breathing became irregular as incoherent thoughts tumbled through her mind.

"Only one." Randall heard her own words and for an instant wanted to call them back.

Megan felt mild surprise at Randall's remark. She had not asked the question expecting information; it had been purely rhetorical. "And did you touch her?" She locked eyes with Randall, wanting information.

"No, I was afraid to. Afraid of her reaction. Afraid of my own feelings. Afraid of where it might lead." Randall felt as if she were falling uncontrollably. She was aware of only two desires — one to fight desperately to stop the fall, the other to surrender to it.

"Were you married at the time?" Megan asked.

"Yes," Randall managed to say.

"Is the woman gay?"

54

"The woman is definitely gay." Randall's voice was almost a whisper.

No longer able to contain her feelings, she slowly leaned forward and brushed her fingertips across Megan's lips. She felt Megan tense, then move forward ever so slightly in response. Rising to her knees, her body within inches of Megan, she placed her lips lightly on Megan's. She moved with deliberate slowness, softly kissing Megan's eyes and returning again gently to kiss her mouth.

Excitement, desire, and fear moved through her body. Her heart was beating rapidly, she knew she wanted more than these few kisses.

"Randall." Megan's tone was quiet, commanding. "Do you understand what you're doing?"

"I've wanted to do this for days." Randall's voice was barely above a whisper. Her eyes were riveted on Megan's, and she made no effort to conceal her desire.

She inhaled deeply as Megan's arms gathered her in. Her lips parted easily as she felt Megan's mouth on hers, the warm softness of her tongue as it reached gently inside. Her hands moved lovingly over Megan's back and shoulders. Muscles tensed beneath her fingers as she pressed her mouth against Megan's lips. A heart beat against her breast, Megan's heart.

The sound of violin music hung in the warm air like fine perfume. It filled the room with velvety softness and melted into their embrace.

Randall brushed her lips lightly against Megan's cheek and returned slowly to the softness of her mouth. Her lips spoke warmth and tenderness — a lover's request — free of all demands.

Hands moved beneath Randall's sweater and caressed her breasts. Nipples already firm in response to Megan's kiss stiffened at Megan's touch. Randall was floating now, intoxicated with her own desire.

55

Then, suddenly, without a sound, Megan moved her hands away and separated her body from Randall's.

"What's wrong?" Randall breathed.

Megan's eyes were glassy with desire. "I just remembered that you're married. You're committed to someone else."

Randall's eyes never left Megan's. She felt the wet warmth of tears roll down her cheeks. "I love you, Megan. I didn't mean to, but I do." Randall leaned forward and kissed Megan very lightly on the lips.

The glow from the fire encircled them. Randall sat transfixed as patterns of dark and bright moved against Megan's face. She traced Megan's hands and fingers with her own. A surgeon's hands with long, delicate fingers. Hands that now held her heart.

"Megan, I don't know what will happen tomorrow, next week, or next year. I've never made love with a woman. I don't even know how." She squeezed Megan's hands. "I'm in love with you. And God knows I want to make love with you. I can't look at you without wanting to touch you, without wanting to feel your mouth on mine. It's like a physical pain. I can't ignore it any more. Even if we never make love, I have to tell you what I'm feeling." Her gaze held Megan tenderly. "I want to be close to you in ways I've never shared with anyone else." Her eyes melted into Megan's. "Make love with me, Megan." Her voice was a husky whisper.

Megan's eyes took hold of Randall. Her arms pulled her close and then lowered her gently down to the soft Alpaca rug. Her head bent to Randall, her mouth was soft and sweet against Randall's lips. Her hands embraced, caressed her full breasts and erect nipples. Pleasure moved again and followed the path of Megan's hands. Gentle, skillful hands. Hands more sensual for the trembling passion that moved through them.

A log shifted on the fire, sparks shot into the air, burned bright and disappeared.

"I want to feel you against my skin," Megan murmured, as her tongue caressed Randall's ear. She pulled Randall's sweater off in one continuous movement, then slid other clothing over Randall's hips, letting it fall in a soft heap on the floor.

Randall watched with mounting desire as Megan removed her own sweater. She reached up and traced the firelight already caressing Megan's breasts. Megan stood, and let the rest of her clothing fall from her body.

For a moment time was frozen for Randall. Spellbound by the strength of her own desire, she caressed Megan's body with her eyes. The pliant softness of their skin met and rejoyced as Megan's body covered hers completely. The fresh scent of Megan's skin overwhelmed her senses. Desire spun in her brain like a child's top gone wild. Randall knew only the barest sensation of weight as Megan brushed her skin with her own.

So this is how a woman feels. A passing thought as she closed her eyes, as she reached up and pulled Megan firmly against her, and fell into her own pleasure.

Kisses, slow and hot, blazed a path along her body. They moved downward, leaving memories of their fire behind. Kisses caressed her legs and inner thighs. She shivered as Megan's warm breath washed over her and the exquisite sensations began. Points of sensations that moved outward like ripples on a pond. Rings of pleasure moving from a fiery center, bringing warmth to every part of her. She surrendered to the flame as the strokes of Megan's tongue grew more intense. The sound of her own breathing filled Randall's ears. Rapid, shallow breaths, interrupted by faint murmuring sounds. Sounds of pleasure.

Her hand found Megan's hair and buried itself in it's softness. She pushed Megan's head hard against her and pleasure gave birth to ecstasy. It filled her, held her,

57

surrounded her. Still the strokes continued. Hard, rapid strokes, pushing her higher and higher, exploding her body and mind into thousands of tiny flames. Flames that seared her very soul.

"Stop. Oh God, Megan, stop!" Her hands took Megan's head away.

Randall covered Megan's mouth, hot and wet, with her own. Her lips moved across the wetness, savoring the taste of their love.

"It tastes so good," Randall breathed into Megan's lips, "so very sweet." Her arms pulled Megan closer.

As she listened to the sounds of their breathing, her hand caressed Megan's hair and face. She could feel the warmth of the fire on Megan's skin. Then Megan's warm hair and cheek lay against Randall's breast; lips touched her nipple and warm breath flowed against it.

"You're a wonderful lover, Megan. Do all women make love like that?"

Megan kissed her nipple and raised her head to look at Randall. The firelight glowed golden on her skin. "I don't know about all women."

"You know what I mean." Randall rested a finger against Megan's lips.

"I would guess the mechanics are pretty much the same. The love is different." She kissed Randall's fingers and enclosed them in a warm hand. "Maybe I'm old-fashioned, but I believe it's the closeness the two people share that creates the joy." She brushed Randall's fingers with her lips. "There's a great difference between making love and sharing sex." She looked tenderly into Randall's eyes. "I made love to you, Randall."

Randall's arms encircled Megan's neck, and she pulled her mouth to her own. Her kiss was tender at first. Long, slow, and tender. She moved her hands to Megan's breasts as she rolled gently over her.

"Your skin is so smooth. Soft. Not at all like a man's." Her breathing quickened as desire grew inside her. Her mouth was unsure at first. Then her mind recalled the map left by Megan and her lips followed the memory.

Her mouth moved with loving care, traveling slowly, tasting the warm softness of Megan's skin. Purring sounds came from Randall as she brushed her face and hair along the satin smoothness of Megan's inner thighs. Her body shivered with excitement as her tongue touched the inner sweetness and moved slowly against the silken folds.

The smooth wetness against her tongue, the rosy lips, the warm musk fragrance, the delicious taste of salt and sweetness, the soft murmuring sounds — her senses were filled with Megan. Her eyes closed as her fingers entered Megan. She was stunned by the soft warmth that encircled her.

She moved instinctively, and with each movement she felt Megan's body respond with pleasure. She was intoxicated by her own power. A power to move another human being to a state of obvious joy. To touch a woman and know exactly what pleasure she created. To touch a woman and know the fire that had consumed her own body moments before now burned in this woman's soul.

A loud cry echoed in the room. Randall felt Megan's body tremble, grow rigid. Then hands were pulling Randall's body upward, and Megan's lips were on hers as Megan's arms closed around her.

She looked at Megan with a child's pleasure in what she had just done. "I made love to you, Megan. Not sex, love."

"I know." Megan drew her closer and kissed her.

The fire crackled and popped its warmth into the room. It covered them like a soft blanket as they drifted into sleep.

* * * * *

Megan awakened at four-fifteen. The fireplace was dark, the moon gave the only light as it fell into the chilly room. Megan moved her arm carefully from beneath Randall's head and sat up. She got a soft quilt from the sofa and knelt beside Randall. Moonlight fell on Randall like delicate lace. Megan bent and kissed her forehead. She brushed Randall's hair away from her face and gently kissed her mouth. "Randall." She spoke softly.

Randall stirred and opened her eyes. Without a word she put her arms around Megan's neck, drew her to herself, and kissed her with great tenderness.

"It wasn't a dream," she said as she held Megan's face close to her own.

"It wasn't a dream." Megan smiled. "Let's go upstairs."

They held the quilt around their naked bodies as they climbed the stairs to Megan's room.

Chapter 12

Sunday morning Randall opened her eyes to a sun-drenched room and found herself alone in Megan's bed. She stretched and propped herself against the pillow. As sleep cleared, she heard the sound of the shower.

She got out of bed and soundlessly pushed the bathroom door open. Music was coming from a radio inside the shower, Kenny Rogers singing "Lady." Randall listened for a moment, watching the outline of Megan's body silhouetted against the translucent glass, following the outline of Megan's hand as she moved a bar of soap across her shoulders. She watched in silence, feeling the stirrings of desire. Her breathing changed; there was a wetness between her thighs.

Randall opened the door and stepped inside.

Megan turned to her. "You were sound asleep a few minutes ago." Her eyes burned into Randall. "I was planning to wake you when I finished."

"I'm awake now." Randall's eyes moved over Megan. Her body looked even softer as streams of water made their way in meandering courses from head to foot. Sunshine entered through a large skylight, bathed the streams and gave a glistening quality to Megan's skin.

Pale gray desire caressed Randall's body and locked itself firmly on her eyes.

"Are you going to come over here," Megan said, "or should I move over there?"

Without a word, Randall came toward Megan. As warm rain fell against her skin, her excitement rose.

Megan's voice was soft. "I'll wash you."

She moved her soap-lathered hands slowly over Randall's shoulders, caressing her breasts, taking the nipples between her fingers and squeezing them gently. Her lips came to Randall's, and she brushed them with the tip of her tongue. Megan slid her arms around Randall and pulled her to herself. Warm streams found new paths as their bodies joined together, wet skin more slippery than satin.

Megan's tongue pushed its way into Randall's mouth and was met with raw passion, Randall's kiss hard and intense. She caught Megan's tongue and pulled it more deeply into her, her mouth moving roughly over Megan's.

Megan felt her own passion ignite as Randall guided her hand between her thighs.

"I want you," Randall breathed as she pushed Megan's hand harder against herself.

Megan's eyes were pale gray flames fueled by her own desire. Randall pushed her body tightly against Megan. Her tongue entered Megan's mouth a second before she felt

Megan's fingers inside her. She slid her own hand between Megan's thighs and buried herself within.

They stood braced against each other, mouths locked in embrace, fingers moving in mirrored motion and tempo.

Megan felt warm water on her tongue as she opened her mouth wider to breathe. Her legs were trembling as a steady stream of pleasure moved outward from Randall's fingers and climbed her body like a flame. Her own excitement had grown faster than Randall's, but she resisted as Randall's free hand moved to her fingers to push them away.

"You first." Randall licked warm streams on Megan's face and slid Megan's fingers out of her.

Megan's arms were around Randall's shoulders. Leaning against the smooth tile, she felt her knees buckle as Randall's fingers moved deeper and faster. Megan collapsed against her, waves of pleasure turning her body liquid. A second wave broke over her, and she dissolved to her knees.

Randall followed her, never losing contact.

Slowly she withdrew her fingers and wrapped her arms around Megan. She lifted Megan's face to hers and ran her tongue along the inside of her mouth.

Megan's hands were on Randall's breasts, the nipples stiff between Megan's fingers. "Come, sit over here." Megan motioned toward a marble seat in the far corner of the shower.

Randall sat down and raised her lips to Megan. Megan's tongue moved against hers in sharp, strong thrusts. Megan's hands slid between her thighs to separate them; then her mouth moved to the smooth satin folds. Gasping with pleasure, Randall opened her legs wider and pushed Megan's mouth more firmly against her.

Megan moved even faster. Randall's fingers dug into her shoulders as she cried out in pleasure.

Her body relaxe; she lifted Megan's face and drew it to hers. Her kisses were gentle now, tender touches, speaking love.

Randall grinned into Megan's eyes. "You're as good at sex as you are at making love."

Just as they were going back to bed, the phone rang. Megan caught it on the third ring. A few minutes later she hung up and turned to Randall. "That was the hospital in Atlanta. I have to go back right away."

"I thought someone was covering for you."

"For everything but this. They have a heart donor for a patient. I'm a member of the transplant team."

Randall got up and put her arms around Megan. "I'm happy for the patient but disappointed that we won't have more time."

"There'll be other times."

"Is there a plane out soon?"

"The hospital is arranging for a private jet to be at a field about fifteen minutes from here." Megan looked wistfully at Randall. "I'm sorry. Do you want to stay and ski?"

"Not without you. When do we leave?"

"As soon as we're packed." Megan looked at her watch. "Which will have to be fast."

Chapter 13

Less than an hour later they were in the air, headed for Atlanta, the only passengers on a small Lear jet.

"At least I have you to myself up here." Randall smiled at Megan. "I had a wonderful time, just not long enough."

"One of the drawbacks of cardiology is that just about everything has to be done yesterday."

"I can live with that." Randall squeezed Megan's hand. "Hey, I'm just glad they didn't call an hour earlier. That would have been unforgivable."

Megan laughed. "Believe me, it's been known to happen. And you're right, it's unforgivable."

"And I thought I was special?" Randall said with pretended hurt. "You've been interrupted before."

"You are special. The interruptions before were with Ellen." Megan's face was serious. "You're the first person I've made love with in fourteen months. In fact, you're the first person I've so much as kissed in fourteen months."

"I feel very lucky. If someone had told me months or even weeks ago that I'd be in love with you today, I'd have told them they were crazy." She lifted Megan's hand and kissed the back of her fingers.

"You're not the only surprised person on this plane. I hadn't the slightest intention of becoming involved with anyone, let alone an attorney whose greatest pleasure in life seemed to be harassing me about contracts and lease agreements."

Randall looked directly into Megan's eyes. "Believe me, that isn't my greatest pleasure in life." Randall's smile faded, and Megan could see the softness in her eyes. "I really love you, Megan. More than I would have believed possible."

"I can't tell you yet that I'm in love with you, Randall." Megan spoke very gently. "But I could be." She leaned over and kissed Randall softly. "I've had more fun and felt more alive this weekend than I have in more than a year."

"I hope this trip was only the beginning. I want to spend a lot of time with you."

"I'm counting on it. But my work is very demanding; you may not find it easy dealing with my schedule. Although today was highly unusual," Megan conceded. "We do an average of two heart transplants a year."

"So one of them has to happen today," Randall grumbled. "How come I've never seen you interviewed on television?" Her question was partly serious, partly in jest.

"Heart transplants aren't that unusual anymore, unless an artificial heart is used to replace the real one. Besides, I'm only a member of the team, not the lead surgeon, and I'm glad to have it that way. I don't even like cocktail parties, much less TV interviews." Megan's gray eyes were bright with sincerity.

"How long will you be?" Randall asked. "I'd be happy to fix you a late supper."

Megan shook her head. "Impossible. Heart transplants go on for hours on end. And once the surgery is completed, I practically live at the hospital for a few days. If I make it home at all, it will be for a change of clothes — and most likely my office staff will pick those up for me."

Randall smiled, her gaze drifting down Megan's trim body. "I can see that I have a lot to learn about the life and times of a heart surgeon."

"Well, I have every confidence in you, Counselor. You're a very fast learner."

"Thank you, I try."

Chapter 14

It was five days before Megan was able to do more than speak with Randall by phone. The surgery had gone flawlessly, but a slight lung infection had kept Megan on constant call. With the patient's condition finally stabilized, Megan met Randall for lunch.

"Can you have dinner with me tomorrow night?" Megan asked as soon as they had ordered their salads.

"I have to go to New York tonight on business," Randall said regretfully. "I'll be there three days. Can you come with me?"

"I'd like to. But I can't," Megan said with equal regret. "Call me the instant you get back?"

"You can count on it." Randall smiled. "I miss you already."

* * * * *

When Randall returned home, she was surprised to find Kenneth packing his suitcase.

"Where are you going?"

"To New York with you. I have business there, and there's no reason I can't get it done while you have to be there, too."

"Kenneth, I'm going to be very busy with depositions." She felt resentful. "There won't be a lot of time for socializing."

"My dear, I'm not going to New York to socialize. You know me better than that. It just so happens that our schedules work out together for a change." Kenneth looked at Randall: "Is there a problem?"

"No, not really," she said hastily, defensively. "You know I don't like mixing business with pleasure. I just don't want you to expect a vacation with me when I'm going to work."

The phone rang, and Kenneth picked it up. "It's for you." He handed the phone to Randall and walked into the other room. "I have some papers to get ready."

Randall was surprised to hear Megan's voice. "I hope I'm not interrupting," Megan said.

"Of course you're not interrupting. It's good to hear your voice."

"I thought about your invitation to go with you to New York. I'd like to go. I think I can get someone to cover for me."

Randall was silent for a moment, her mind churning with thought.

"Randall?" Megan said. "Is there something wrong?"

"Yes, Kenneth is going with me. He has business there and has decided to get it done while I'm there."

"Oh." Megan felt embarrassed. She had not expected this complication. "Well, maybe another time."

"Megan, I'm sorry. I had no idea he was going. I can't see any way to change his mind."

69

"Don't worry about it. I'll see you when you get back."

"Megan, I'd much rather be going with you. Believe me, this will not be a pleasure trip."

"It's okay, Randall. Things happen." Megan exerted effort to sound casual. "Have a good trip, and call me when you get back."

"I'll miss you," Randall said.

Megan sat in mild shock. It had been too easy to get caught up in her feelings for Randall. She had never seen Randall with Kenneth, had never met Kenneth. Now she had a voice to put with his name. She was not going to New York with Randall because Kenneth was going. Suddenly Randall's marriage was very real. The thought settled into Megan's consciousness: *You're involved with a married woman who is living with, and sleeping with, her husband.*

She spoke out loud. "Megan McKenzie, you're a fool."

Chapter 15

"Well," Lynn Bradley said as she settled herself comfortably onto one of the sofas. She had telephoned Megan at her office and invited herself for the evening. "So tell me about your trip. Were you terribly lonely without me?"

Megan sighed and took a long swallow of coffee. "Not exactly. I had company. Randall Grayson went along."

"I might have guessed," Lynn said. She noticed that Megan wasn't looking at her. "Megan, is there something wrong?"

"You might say that." Megan got up and stood in front of the fire with her back to Lynn. The warmth comforted her slightly, and she was aware of the hickory fragrance.

Lynn watched Megan closely. She was concerned by the discomfort Megan conveyed. "Meggie, what is it?"

Megan turned and looked at Lynn.

Lynn felt anger as the one thought she didn't want to deal with entered her mind. "My God, you slept with her. Didn't you?"

Megan sat opposite Lynn. "Worse than that."

"What's worse? You certainly didn't get her pregnant."

"Lynn, this is serious. Randall says she's in love with me. I'm not in love with her yet, but I could be."

Lynn felt the blood drain from her face. Her lips closed to a narrow line. "Don't be ridiculous. You don't even know her."

Megan got up and began to pace. "I'm not talking 'want to spend my life with someone' love. I'm talking 'in love, want to be with someone' love." Megan flopped down on the sofa opposite Lynn. "I'm terribly attracted to her — that kind of thing." She looked at Lynn. "Damn it, Lynn, you know what I'm saying — I'm sexually attracted to her."

"You're infatuated with her, you want to continue going to bed with her. Wouldn't that be a more accurate description?" Lynn's tone was acid. She fought to maintain control as jealousy and anger exploded in her. The thought of Megan in bed with someone, wanting someone. . . .

"Don't be a bitch," Megan chided her. "It's more than sex. I enjoy her company. She has a good mind and a good sense of humor."

"You sound like a teenager. Damn it, Megan, do you have any idea what you could be into here? What if she tells her husband? Do you think he's going to say, That's fine, dear, I'd love to meet the woman, let's have her over for dinner?"

Megan recapped her telephone conversation with Randall.

"Lovely!"

"Lynn, your sarcasm doesn't help,"Megan said with a trace of anger. "I repeat, I know I have a problem."

"What problem? Don't see her again. That ends the problem." She could feel her temples pounding. She wanted

72

to scream at Megan, to grab her by the shoulders and shake her. It took all of her professional control to keep her voice even. She could not, however, keep the sarcasm out of her tone.

Megan got up, knelt by Lynn, and took her hand. "I know you're angry with me, but your anger is getting in the way right now. Please,hear me."

Megan looked into Lynn's eyes. "I haven't had a chance to talk to Randall about how I feel. I don't know what her plans are. She may want out of her marriage. But I won't know for sure until I talk to her."

"Would it make that much difference if she *were* getting a divorce?" Lynn asked quietly. Her heart raced in anticipation of the dreaded answer.

"Probably. At least I wouldn't feel quite so guilty and quite so stupid. Right now, I feel like I jumped into a pool without checking to see if it had any water in it."

"Megan, even if she *is* planning a divorce,you're in for a rough trip. Divorce is always messy. What if you get named as a correspondent, sued for alienation of affection?" Lynn felt desperate. "That could really hurt your career. You've worked too hard. . . ." Lynn hesitated for a moment, then continued. "Has she ever been involved with a woman before?"

"No, I'm the first."

"If you get involved too deeply, you're bound to get hurt."

"I'm already involved," Megan said simply. "There's no way I can get out of this without some pain."

Lynn looked at Megan with great tenderness; she had loved this woman for too many years. "I think I know what you mean." She forced a smile. "The best I can offer is to advise you to talk with her candidly when she gets back. Make your feelings clear, and listen to her response." She said with effort, "If you two have something worth fighting for, then fight. But

Megan, if you're only an experience for her, cut your losses and run. Go on with your life."

She looked deeply into Megan's eyes. "I'll be happy to administer emergency care for any trauma incurred." Her light blue eyes were warm with affection.

"You're a good friend, Lynn. I care about you very much."

Would that the word was "love," instead of "care," Lynn thought.

Chapter 16

Randall and Kenneth took a taxi from LaGuardia. Mounds of dirty snow from a storm two days earlier were piled like borders around buildings and on curbs; the traffic and time had turned the patches of white into tattle-tale gray and soot black.

The lobby of the Excelsior Hotel was crowded. A convention of dentists was in the process of checking in, and it took twenty minutes before Randall and Kenneth were shown to their room.

"What a madhouse!" Kenneth said as he tipped the bellman and closed the door.

"It was your idea to come along. I told you it wasn't a pleasure trip," Randall said testily, thinking of Megan. She opened her suitcase and began hanging clothes in the closet.

The room had one king-sized bed — the dentists had booked all of the double rooms. Dingy floor-to-ceiling drapes framed a view of gray rooftops.

"Would you like to get something to eat?" Randall asked, looking intently at Kenneth. He was sitting on the bed with his back propped against two pillows. "Are you all right, Kenneth? You look awfully pale."

"I have indigestion. I don't think I could eat a bite. I'd just like to stay here and relax."

"I'll call room service. Are you sure you don't want something?"

"A soft drink would be good. Maybe it would help this pain in my chest."

Randall ordered a club sandwich and two Cokes. The food arrived thirty minutes later, and Randall ate her sandwich as they watched a cable news station.

"Randall," Kenneth said suddenly.

Randall turned and looked at her husband. His face was ashen gray, his breathing labored.

"What's wrong?" Randall moved quickly to the bed.

"A crushing pain . . . in my chest. My left arm . . . I think I'm having a heart attack."

Randall picked up the phone. She spoke urgently to the front desk, explaining. "Please, hurry!"

She sat on the edge of the bed. "Why don't you lie down?"

"I don't think . . . I can breathe lying down." He held his hand to the middle of his chest. "This . . . is really bad."

There was a knock on the door, a shout: "Hotel doctor!"

Moments later the bearded young doctor said tersely, "We need to get him to a hospital immediately."

Before he could reach for the phone, two paramedics pushed a stretcher into the room.

"Myocardial infarction," the doctor stated. "I've given him a shot of Lidocaine."

Randall, stunned, frozen into silence, rode in the ambulance and held Kenneth's hand during the fifteen-minute ride to Manhattan General Hospital. She was waved to a waiting room while an emergency room physician examined Kenneth, and then admitted him to the cardiac intensive care unit.

Randall felt nauseous as she paced the CIC waiting room. Forty minutes later a tall, gray-haired man entered and introduced himself as Doctor Jarvis.

"Your husband has suffered an acute angina attack. He'll be fine, but we'd like to keep him in the hospital for a couple of days to run some tests and make sure there's been no damage to the heart muscle."

" Can I see him?" Randall asked.

"For a few minutes. He's pretty groggy. We've sedated him."

Kenneth looked smaller and very helpless in the hospital bed. Pulsating light monitored his heartbeat on a small screen above his head.

Randall took his hand. "The cardiologist says you'll be fine. In just a few more days I can take you home."

Kenneth's eyelids were half closed. "I thought I was going to die." His speech was slightly slurred. "All I could think about was not spending enough time with you." His eyes closed, then fluttered open again. "I love you." He squeezed her hand.

Randall bent and kissed Kenneth on the forehead. "I'll be back first thing in the morning."

Kenneth fought to hold his eyes open. "We have to spend more time together." His eyes closed, and he drifted into sleep.

It was ten forty-five when Randall arrived at the hotel. She went straight to her room and telephoned Megan.

"God, I'm glad you're home," Randall said as she heard Megan's voice. "Kenneth is in the hospital, an acute angina attack. They have him in intensive care."

"Which hospital?" Megan was immediately authoritative.

"Manhattan General. The doctor wants to keep him for a few days, run some tests. . . ."

"Would you like me to call and see what I can find out?"

"I'd appreciate that." Randall took a deep breath. "He looked so gray, he scared me to death."

"I wish I were there with you. Do you want me to fly up?"

"You're sweet! If he has to be in the hospital long, I may take you up on it. If he really does get out in a couple of days, we'll fly back to Atlanta immediately."

"If you change your mind, call me. I can get someone to cover for me and be there in a couple of hours."

"I love you," Randall said. "Will you call me after you talk to Kenneth's doctor?"

"I'll call him first thing in the morning. If I don't get you at the hotel, you call me."

"Thanks, I miss you," Randall said softly.

"I'm glad," Megan said. "Sleep warm."

Chapter 17

Kenneth was discharged from the hospital two days later.

"God, it feels good to be outside again," he said to Randall as he walked gingerly to the waiting taxi.

"It feels good knowing that your heart has no permanent damage," Randall said.

"Whatever the doctors call it, it sure started me thinking."

Kenneth reached for Randall's hand. Her fingers felt taken by surprise as he wrapped his large hand around hers.

"For a while I thought I was going to die. All I could think about — even more than being scared — was that I hadn't spent enough time with you."

He looked at Randall and saw the surprise she could not conceal.

* * * * *

The flight left exactly on time, a fact that delighted Kenneth. The aircraft leveled off and the flight attendants served drinks and peanuts. "Back to what I was telling you in the taxi," Kenneth said. He reached again for Randall's hand. Randall squeezed his fingers and lifted her hand free, using both hands to tear open the package of peanuts.

"We should spend more time together," Kenneth repeated. "It's time to start a family. If we're going to have kids, this would be a perfect age for both of us."

"What about your work? You're out of town three weeks every month," Randall said, alarm fluttering within her. "I don't think you should have to sacrifice your career for a child at this point. We have plenty of time to start a family."

"That's just it. I don't want to put it off any longer. I'm going to talk to Jordan about less travel and more local cases. I'm a senior partner, so I should have the right to make that choice. I've paid my dues with the firm. It's about time I paid more attention to us."

"Kenneth, what you're talking about is an awfully big step. I'm not sure I'm ready for a child right now." She smiled. "I'd still like to be a senior partner myself."

"We don't need extra income. We have plenty of money. In fact, you don't have to work at all unless you really want to." Kenneth's voice was excited. "We could have a child, and you could take off a year or so to be with the baby."

"I don't *want* to quit my job." She looked into his animated face with resentment. "I put a lot of time and energy into law school. I'm not willing to walk away from a career when I'm just getting started."

"Okay, I can understand that." He spread his hands in a placating gesture. "We can still have a child. We can hire a nurse, a nanny, whatever they call them. That way you could

80

go back to work right away." He was obviously pleased with himself. "I know I've surprised you with this — but give it some thought. We'll talk about it again in a few more days."

"I don't think a few more days will change my mind, Kenneth." She spoke adamantly. "I'm just not interested in starting a family right now."

"Well, I'm going to talk to Jordan about less travel anyway," he replied. "You'll change your mind about a family."

"I doubt it." Randall took a long swallow from her soft drink.

"Give yourself time. We get along fine in every way — why shouldn't we have a family? We have a pretty good sex life, it's only natural that we'd want children."

"You're not *listening* to me. I don't want children right now. I want a career." Remembering his angina attack, she tried to control her emotions, but anger spilled into her words. She hissed, "As far as our sex life goes, it has always been mediocre at best. And I stress the words *sex life*. We don't make love. To use your phrase, we have sex. Two-thirds of the time I don't even reach orgasm. That does not rate with me as an okay sex life."

"You haven't complained before." His pale blue eyes looked into hers with astonishment. "Why haven't you said something?"

She looked back at him in exasperation. "God, Kenneth, I tried talking to you a hundred times the first year we were married. You were either on your way to court, or deep in a brief, or you told me our sex life would improve with time — that I just needed to get used to you. Don't you recall *any* of those conversations? Because I sure as hell do." Randall knew her face was red.

"I was wrong." His voice was flat, his eyes contrite. "I want to change things."

"Damn it, Kenneth, why now? Why all of a sudden? You're not dying."

"I guess this heart thing got me to realize there are more important things in life than a career. My work just isn't enough to make me happy."

"Well, it's not up to me to make you happy. Up till now you haven't given much thought at all to whether I'm happy."

Kenneth shook his head. "I plead guilty on all counts. But it can't be too late to change. Randall . . . give us a chance."

She said bluntly, "I'm not sure I want us to change."

Kenneth leaned back and looked at her. "I'm not going to ask if you're involved with someone." His voice had changed, had become granite. "At this point I don't want to know. But let me give you a word of advice. Don't deny me a child because you're playing games on the side. And don't let me find out you're playing around. You wouldn't like the consequences."

"Don't you threaten me," she hurled her words, astonished by this unsuspected side of him.

"I want a child. It's just that simple. I want a son to carry on my name." Kenneth's eyes were as hard as coal. "What I'm saying isn't a threat — it's a promise."

Chapter 18

Randall had known Pat Martin since their law school days at Harvard. They had become immediate and close friends, sharing confidences with ease, had remained good friends, meeting for dinner at least once a month, talking frequently by telephone. Pat's office was only two blocks from Randall's and Randall met her for lunch at a nearby restaurant.

"You sounded desperate on the phone. Is there trouble at the office or on the homefront?" As usual, Pat got right to the point.

"Kenneth has decided to change his lifestyle," Randall said succinctly. "He wants us to get closer and start a family."

Pat grinned. She was an attractive woman with shoulder-length auburn hair and large blue eyes. "Don't you want a Kenneth Junior?"

"Pat, I'm serious. He's talking to Jordan today about taking more in-town cases and cutting back drastically on his travel. I could kill him." Randall's eyes were bright with anger.

"Ah! There's more to this than meets the ear." Pat put down her fork and leaned toward Randall. "Tell me the rest. Why are you so upset? Are you involved with someone? What's his name, and what does he do?"

"I am involved, but I wouldn't be interested in raising a family even if I weren't. Let's face it. Kenneth and I are not parent material. If he weren't panicking over his medical problems, he'd be the first to admit it."

"True, the thought of a little Kenneth running around is enough to make my blood run cold, *but*," Pat returned to her question, "tell me about the new man in your life."

Randall leaned back in her chair and grinned. "It's not a man. It's a woman."

Pat, in the middle of swallowing some iced tea, choked. She held up her napkin and took another sip to ease her throat. "You devil, you." She grinned widely. "You'll try anything. Same old Randall."

Randall said primly, "I have never been involved with a woman before."

"That's about the only thing you missed while we were in law school." Pat took another drink of iced tea. "Where did you meet her? What does she do? And is she any good in bed?"

"She's a client at the firm. She's a physician, and she's very bright and interesting."

"And? Come on, tell all. Is she a good lover?"

Randall smiled. "She's fantastic!"

"You lucky dog. No wonder you don't want Kenneth hanging around."

"That's only part of it. This woman is a very decent person. She believes in long-term relationships."

"What's wrong with that? Hell, if she's all that wonderful, why would you want to get rid of her?"

I don't want to get rid of her. I'm in love with her. I'm considering leaving Kenneth."

"Are you *crazy?*" Her smile fading, Pat stared at her. "Having an affair with a woman is one thing, living with a female lover is another. Society does not look kindly on lesbians. That's what you'd be considered if you left Kenneth for her." Pat added emphatically, "You'd be a *lesbian*. If your firm found out, you'd be out the door. God, can you imagine Jordan's reaction if he knew? He'd want to have you burned at the stake." She laughed nervously.

"This isn't funny," Randall retorted. "I really care about her. I'm not in love with Kenneth. I think I could have a decent life with her."

"Randall, since I've known you, you have really cared for about at least a dozen men. The infatuation lasted for a while, and when the sex was no longer new, the guy was no longer interesting. What makes this so different — that it's a woman? The difference that can make if it were to get out, you wouldn't like."

She leaned across the table and said earnestly, "Take my advice. Keep the lady on the side as long as it's fun, but don't give up Kenneth. Kenneth affords an air of respectability that your lady friend can never offer you. In our profession, propriety is important. If you left Kenneth for a woman, you'd be ruined. No firm would have you. Not to mention the fact that Kenneth would take you to the cleaners financially. No man's ego is strong enough to survive the fact that he's been dropped for a woman."

"I'm not in love with Kenneth." Randall said stubbornly. "I am in love with Megan. Why should I live a lie?"

"You never were in love with Kenneth. You married him because of what he could do for your career. You've lived a lie this long, you'd better continue to live that lie."

"I don't want children," Randall argued, "and I won't give Megan up."

"Randall, you're a smart woman. Use your head. You can stay on the pill — Kenneth doesn't have to know. Hide the damn things. Hide the lady, too. Meet her at her place, or out of town. As long as you're keeping Kenneth happy, he's not going to be checking up on your extracurricular activities."

"And what do I tell Megan?"

"You tell her you love her, but you can't leave your husband. Tell her he's sick, or that he'll kill you both if you leave. Hell, you'll think of something," Pat said confidently. "You've got the best of both worlds: social acceptance, respectability, a good job — and a lover on the side that you're crazy about. What more could you want? Just don't mess it up with romantic heroics."

"I guess you're right," Randall conceded reluctantly.

"Randall, I know at least five women who are doing exactly what I'm advising you to do, and they're perfectly happy. Believe me, a female lover is one thing, but you are not cut out for a gay lifestyle."

"I'll keep that in mind."

"One other thing." Pat grinned. "When you get tired of this woman, please introduce her to me. She sounds fascinating!"

"She is." Randall smiled. "So don't hold your breath."

Chapter 19

Randall arrived at Megan's house loaded down with gourmet food from La Francaise Delicatessen: smoked turkey, cold boiled shrimp, lobster, marinated mushrooms, pasta salad, other delicacies packed into three large bags.

"I thought it would be nice to eat here," Randall said as she set the bags down in the kitchen. She put her arms around Megan and kissed her. "I missed you. Can I interest you in a late supper?"

"At the risk of sounding very unromantic, I don't think I could wait. I didn't get any lunch today."

Randall kissed Megan again. "Okay, think of your stomach first."

They ate in the den, the fire adding a glowing warmth to the chilly night air.

Afterward, Megan poured more coffee, watching Randall as she put another log on the fire. The gray slacks fit Randall's slim body perfectly, the burgundy sweater looked soft and warm. Megan rose, drew Randall's face near and kissed her softly. "We need to talk," she said quietly.

"Okay, what would you like to talk about?" Randall felt a stab of fear.

"About us. About you and your husband."

Randall moved off a little to look at Megan. "This sounds serious. Is something wrong?"

"I hope not. But yes, it is serious." She took Randall's hands. "I'm very attracted to you, you already know that. But more than that, I'm falling in love with you. I want to know what the future might hold for us." She held Randall's eyes with her own. "Do you see a future for you and me?"

"Of course I see a future for you and me. I thought you realized that when we were in Aspen."

"Randall, I'm not good at beating around the bush. When I called to accept your invitation to New York, and you told me your husband was going, I felt like an idiot. I've never been in this position before. I've never dated a married woman. I don't like the feeling. I'd like to know where your relationship is with Kenneth — and what you have in mind for us."

Randall understood Megan well enough to know that she would not willingly be involved in a triangle. She didn't want to lie to Megan, but she didn't want to lose her either.

"Megan, I love you. You already know how attracted I am to you. I want us to have a long-term relationship. I want us to go on and on and on. I don't want you out of my life." Randall paused for breath.

"But I don't hear you saying you'll leave your husband," Megan pointed out. "I want to share my life with *you* — not just with part of you."

88

Randall thought about Pat's advice. It was worth a try to buy time. "I couldn't leave Kenneth now. You know the situation with his health. The doctor said he should avoid stress."

Megan said sharply, "He can live a very long time with angina. It won't kill him."

Randall felt trapped. How foolish of her to use Kenneth's health as an excuse with a cardiologist. "He's scared out of his mind. He believes he could die any minute. He's turned to me for assurance."

Megan's eyes did not leave Randall's. "Does that mean you feel obligated to stay with him?"

"Not forever, but at least until he's used to his new situation. He has to take it easy for a while. He's asked Jordan to let him travel less."

"Randall, are you in love with your husband?"

"No, I'm not. But he is a human being. I just can't walk out on him." Randall felt unbearably pressured. "Surely you can understand that."

Megan felt herself withdraw from Randall. "How long are you planning to stay with him?"

"A few months. Just enough time for him to get back on his feet. We can still see each other while I'm living with Kenneth."

"He certainly doesn't need moths and months. The man isn't recovering from open heart surgery."

Randall accepted the fact that she would have to compromise with Megan. "How long sounds reasonable to you?"

"One month."

"You really think that's enough time?"

"It's twice as long as he needs," Megan stated. "Unless there's another reason you're not telling me."

"There's no other reason." Randall's mind was moving quickly, weighing and discarding ways to deal with Megan's demand. She looked at Megan. "Okay, a month."

Megan smiled broadly. "You'll leave Kenneth in a month?"

"Yes." Randall kissed Megan lightly. "I don't guarantee Kenneth's reaction, but I'll leave him in a month."

"We'll worry about that when it happens. I don't think Kenneth will want a scene any more than we do."

"I'm not sure about that, Megan. Kenneth is a very possessive man. He doesn't like anyone taking something he feels belongs to him."

Megan kissed Randall. "You don't belong to him. He can't possess you. You're mine." She kissed Randall with passion. "Let's go upstairs."

"I thought you'd never ask."

Chapter 20

During the next month, Randall made sure that she saw a lot of Megan. She was at Megan's house frequently, and twice, when Kenneth was out of town, she spent the night. It was a total all-out effort to catch Megan so firmly, involve her so deeply, that she would be unable to hold Randall to their agreement.

For much of that month Megan avoided Lynn. Finally, Lynn cornered her by waiting outside surgery. Megan was only mildly surprised to see Lynn standing there when she walked into the doctors' dressing room.

"You need a new answering service," Lynn chided her.

"Why?" Megan pulled off her surgical cap and shook her hair free.

"Well, apparently they're not giving you your messages."

"I got my messages. I've just been busy." She removed the green surgical gown.

"Then it's about time you got a break. I'll buy you a cup of coffee. Let's go to the cafeteria."

Megan started to make an excuse, but Lynn headed her off: "I warn you, Megan, I won't take no for an answer."

They both laughed.

The cafeteria was nearly empty. They took a corner table, and Megan gave her full attention to her coffee. She added artificial sweetener twice and creamer three times as Lynn watched patiently. As Megan tasted it for the fourth time, Lynn moved the creamer and sweetener to the far side of the table.

"What the hell is going on?" She looked directly into Megan's eyes. "No snow job — the truth."

Megan grimaced. "You won't like it."

"I don't have to like it, Megan. It's your life."

"I've been seeing a lot of Randall for the past couple of weeks. She may be leaving her husband soon."

"When donkeys fly!" Lynn's eyes never moved from Megan's.

"We have an agreement. I gave her a month to move out, or we stop seeing each other. The time is up next Friday."

"I see. So she's been at your place most of the time."

"Yes."

"What happens next Friday?"

"She either moves out, or we break up."

"Break up? You mean you stop seeing her entirely?"

"That's right. She knows what the agreement is."

"Can you do that, Megan? Can you just stop seeing her?"

"If I have to," Megan answered tersely.

"Is she going to move in with you?"

"I hope so."

Lynn felt her heart sink. "That was your idea, wasn't it?"

"Yes, what's wrong with it?" Megan's voice was slightly defensive.

"Not a thing, except I don't think your friend is going to leave her husband."

"We won't know that for sure until next Friday," Megan said with a touch of impatience. "I gave my word. I have to give her that chance."

"Are you ready to extend your agreement? She'll ask for an extension. Will you give it to her?"

"No." Megan's eyes were deadly serious. "There won't be any extensions."

Lynn could read her determination. She knew Megan well enough to know that she meant what she said.

Lynn forced a small smile. "Do me a favor — don't ignore my calls. We've been friends too long for that."

"I'm sorry, I apologize," Megan's light gray eyes focused on Lynn's. "But in return I want you to be less negative about Randall. In fact, I'd like you and Randall to get to know each other. Will you come to dinner tomorrow night?"

"Yes," Lynn replied, suddenly and acutely interested in getting to know Randall Grayson. "I'll be there."

Chapter 21

Lynn settled into a chair in Megan's den. She had talked cordially and smiled through dinner as the three women spoke of books, movies, and skiing. She had watched the poised, witty, and articulate Randall, trying to discern some sign of her real motives, evaluating her every word and action with the heart of a would-be lover, watching her chances for success disappear before her eyes. She took pride only in her certainty that neither her voice nor her face had betrayed her heart.

"Can I get you some brandy or some more coffee?" Megan asked.

"No, thank you. I'm completely content. In fact," Lynn said, looking at her watch, "I'm going to have to leave very soon. I didn't realize we'd talked and eaten our way through three hours."

"I've enjoyed every minute of it," Randall said. "I can understand why Megan thinks so much of you. I hope we can do this often."

Lynn's mind was registering Randall's physical appearance as she listened, the finely chiseled features and the light blue eyes.

"Why don't we get together again next week?" Megan was happy that the evening had gone so smoothly.

"I won't be here next week." Lynn looked at Megan reproachfully. "I'm leaving for San Francisco on Sunday."

"That's right. I forgot about the conference." Megan looked surprised. She added contritely, "I was supposed to go with you."

"I won't hold you to a commitment made six months ago. After all, things have changed since then," Lynn conceded grudgingly.

"Hey, I was looking forward to the trip. I haven't been to San Francisco in years."

"You ought to go," Randall urged.

"I'd like to." Megan's eyes brightened. "I have an idea. Randall, come with us. It'll be fun. The three of us can see the city together."

Lynn was shocked. She couldn't believe that Megan was actually inviting Randall on a trip they had planned together. True, it was a medical convention, but they had planned to explore the city and enjoy the nightlife together.

"It shouldn't be hard to get another airline reservation. If need be, we could leave on a different flight and meet Lynn there." Megan turned to Lynn. "You won't mind flying by yourself, will you?"

Lynn felt a mixture of humiliation and anger. Her mind moved quickly to keep both emotions to herself. "Actually, Megan, you'd have to make a reservation, too. I didn't think you'd want to go, so I asked someone to go with me."

Megan's face changed. "You did? Who?"

"You don't know her. She's a computer programmer. A friend introduced us about a month ago."

Megan's eyes were glued on Lynn in disbelief. "You never mentioned her. How come?"

"As I recall, you've been rather distracted." Lynn smiled, pleased that she had taken Megan by surprise. "Is it important?"

"Not really. I'm just surprised. I didn't know you were seeing anyone."

Lynn looked at Randall. "I'm sure Megan could get reservations if you'd like to go. The four of us could see the city together."

"What's her name?" Megan asked.

"Jill Ryan." Lynn met Megan's eyes. "You've never met, but I know you'll like her. So — how about it, you two — are you coming along?"

Megan had regained her composure. She looked at Randall. "Let's go along. Can you manage the time?"

"Sure. I don't have any court dates scheduled, and Kenneth will be out of town until next Friday." She smiled broadly. "I'd love to go along."

Chapter 22

"What are you doing, roaming around this late?" Jill Ryan asked as she opened the door to Lynn. "I could barely hear you on the phone. Where were you?"

Lynn sat on the sofa and looked at Jill. "I was calling from a phone near the expressway. Believe me, I was glad when you answered."

Jill Ryan was an attractive young woman, with shoulder-length black hair she had inherited from her Chinese mother and almond-shaped blue eyes given her by her Irish father.

Lynn had met Jill almost three years earlier in San Francisco and they had dated for two months before deciding they were not destined to spend a lifetime together. They had, however, remained good friends and had spoken at least once a week by phone. Lynn was delighted when Jill decided to move to Atlanta.

"So tell me what's wrong." Jill watched Lynn's eyes as she listened. "Unexpected visits are not your style."

"I need your help. I want you to go to San Francisco with me on Sunday." Lynn picked up the sofa pillow and fumbled with it as she spoke. "I need you to be my date for the week."

Puzzled but amused, Jill asked, "Any particular reason, or are you just having trouble getting someone to go with you?"

Lynn had confided in Jill on many occasions about her feelings for Megan. She filled Jill in on what had happened at dinner.

"I wasn't about to go as a third wheel. If I wasn't presenting a paper, I'd think of some excuse to cancel." Miserably, Lynn folded her arms around the pillow.

"And I thought my life was complicated on the coast," Jill said with a grin. "You're lucky I don't start work for two weeks. Of course I'll go. I'll be so crazy about you that Megan will have to notice what she's passing up."

"Right now I'll settle for having my own date for the week." Lynn relaxed and let go of the pillow. She grinned at Jill. "You don't have to overdo it. I don't want them to think we're nymphomaniacs."

"Trust me, we Amerasians can be very discreet." Jill winked. "Your secret is safe with me."

Lynn rolled her eyes toward the ceiling. "Right!"

Chapter 23

Megan managed to get seats on Lynn's flight, and the four arrived in San Francisco together. After settling into adjoining rooms at the Mark Hopkins, they set out to see the city; Jill acting as guide, showing them the Castro, Valencia Street, and other gay areas of the city not on the usual sightseeing tours. They looked back as they climbed the hills and watched the cable cars throw static sparks into the cool air.

They had accepted a dinner invitation at the home of two of Lynn's friends, and during the drive to Sausalito the glistening city unfolded for them as they crossed the Bay Bridge.

"I know you'll like Vivian and Carroll," Lynn said. "They've been together for twenty years. Vivian is a psychiatrist and Carroll renovates old houses." Lynn was glancing in the rear view mirror at Megan and Randall. They were sitting much closer than she liked.

"Does Carroll have her own business?" Megan asked.

Lynn nodded. "Three other women work with her, and she's right in there with them, ripping out walls and redesigning the floor plans." She glanced in the rear view mirror again. "She's a very sharp business woman. I wish they lived in Atlanta, but you couldn't blast either of them away from the Bay area. We're just about there."

The house was a large contemporary structure that grew up out of a cliff, its large cathedral windows giving an unimpaired view of the ocean moving below like a living creature rubbing its back against the rocks.

Carroll Lassiter could easily have fit into an ad promoting skiing in Switzerland. Her short, curly blonde hair and pale blue eyes were accentuated by a deep and even tan, and her smile flashed even white teeth any movie star would have envied.

Vivian Myers, who hugged Lynn as Carroll released her, was a complete contrast to Carroll. She was a delicate woman, about five foot three inches, a full eight inches shorter than Carroll. Her dark hair and olive skin conveyed her Hispanic ancestry.

After a half hour of small talk, Carroll interrupted. "I'm going to get dinner on the table. Lynn, how about giving me a hand?"

Lynn followed Carroll into the kitchen. "What do you want me to do?" she asked.

"Sit down," Carroll ordered her, "and tell me about you and Megan, and why you're both with other people instead of each other."

Lynn tried to maintain a light tone as she told Carroll what had happened in the past several months.

"So, when Ellen was killed about two years ago, it was my turn to be there for Megan," Lynn concluded.

"And when did you fall in love with her?"

"Am I that obvious? I thought I handled it pretty well."

"I don't think someone who didn't know you would pick up on it, but Vivian and I know you pretty well."

Lynn sighed. "I fell in love with her about eighteen months after Joyce died. I'm sure it happened gradually. I'm not one to fall in love on the spot."

"Well, she may very well be infatuated with Randall, but I can tell you that she sure watches you a lot." Carroll grinned. "And her friend is aware of it."

The kitchen door opened and Vivian stuck her head in. "We're starving in here. Where's the food?"

Chapter 24

"Did you enjoy yourself?" Megan asked as she waited for Randall to get into bed.

"Yes, they're all very nice people." Randall slid in beside Megan. "I'm cold, warm me up!" She wrapped her nude body around Megan.

Megan held Randall closely in her arms, savoring the smoothness of her skin. "I've been thinking about this all evening," Megan said.

"Really?" Randall's tone was teasing. "It appeared to me that you were more interested in Lynn. Sure it wasn't Lynn you thought about?"

Megan pulled back and looked at Randall. "Don't be silly. What ever gave you that idea?"

"You watch her an awful lot. I don't think you're even aware of it. Are you sure there's never been anything between you two?"

"Yes, I'm sure." Megan was surprised by the suggestion.

"You were pretty stunned the other night when she told you she was taking someone else to the conference."

"I was surprised, not stunned. Lynn hasn't done much dating in a long time."

"I think you were jealous." Randall's tone was still teasing. "I think you're attracted to Lynn."

"That's ridiculous. Lynn and I have been friends for years. If I were interested in her, we could have had something years ago." She raised her eyebrows. "The woman I'm interested in is right here." She kissed Randall. "In fact, let me show you just how interested."

Megan's hands moved slowly over Randall's breasts. She could feel her own excitement growing as erect nipples pushed against her palms. She traced Randall's lips with her tongue, gently pushing her way inside.

"I love you," Megan spoke into Randall's mouth.

"You want me," Randall whispered.

Megan's breathing increased as she covered Randall's body with her own. Soft smoothness met her skin, yielded to her touch. She met Randall's tongue with quick, darting motions, sucking it inside herself, releasing it, thrusting herself deeper into Randall.

Her hand moved between Randall's legs, fingers trailing a path against her thighs, caressing the satin folds, opening them gently, entering the warm wet softness, caressing the satin walls within.

She moved her mouth slowly down Randall's body, lightly tracing the contours with her tongue, tasting their salty sweetness, delighting in the movements she felt beneath her. Her mouth trailed kisses down Randall's legs and up again, stopping between her thighs, inhaling the warm musk, exhaling her breath against the silk, tracing its folds with a feather's touch, opening her mouth to pull Randall inside, savoring the silky softness with her tongue, holding the pearl gently against her teeth, stroking it more firmly now, aware of her own mounting pleasure as Randall's faint cries grew louder.

Megan felt her own excitement extend from her stomach downward. It spread like a flame, reaching outward and inward with the same movement. She felt herself approaching the edge as the intensity of pleasure inundated her very core.

Randall's hand pushed her head forward, and she increased the speed of her strokes, moving her head from side to side, feeling the silk, and the firm pearl beneath her tongue.

Megan's cries joined with Randall's as she felt her own body convulse, holding Randall firmly now, following her movements with her head. . . . Intensity, ecstasy.

Randall's hands were against her face, lifting it, caressing her mouth, guiding it to her own. Randall's mouth was filled with passion and joy, tasting the passion they shared.

Chapter 25

The first day of the conference went by quickly. Lynn's paper on crisis intervention was so well received that she answered questions for an hour and a half following her presentation. Megan, listening with brimming pride, watched Lynn very closely. In all the years she had known Lynn, she had never heard her speak. Megan wondered why she had never thought of Lynn as attractive, or as the academic type. She smiled as she realized that if she didn't already know Lynn, she would definitely want an introduction. She was beginning to understand what Joyce, and now Jill, saw in Lynn.

Her mind formed the thought: Could Randall be right? Am I jealous of Lynn?

* * * * *

Garbo's was located in a large old house inviting in its warmth and friendliness. The dining room, which formed a horseshoe around a large dance floor and bandstand, was already crowded with couples and groups of women enjoying dinner.

"This is really nice," Lynn commented as they were seated at a table near the dance floor.

"The band starts at eight," Vivian said. "And they're really good. They can play the Big Band sound so well you'd think you were listening to Tommy Dorsey or Glenn Miller."

"I'm surprised this many people turn out for that kind of music," Randall said as she looked around. "I've never seen so many gay people in one place."

"You've never seen this many gay people, period," Megan said, laughing.

"That's true," Randall agreed sheepishly. "I also never thought about black and oriental people being gay."

"We come in all flavors," Jill said with a naughty laugh.

"Atlanta doesn't have the richness of different cultures that you have here," Megan said, looking around the room. "We're growing, but we're no San Francisco."

The band started with "Moonlight Serenade" just as they finished dinner. "One of my favorites," Jill said. "Let's dance, Lynn."

They made their way to the dance floor and melted into the crowd. Megan and Randall soon followed. An hour later, everyone except Lynn and Megan had danced together.

"Are you going to ask Megan to dance?" Vivian asked Lynn as they sat alone at the table.

"Yes, Mother, I am. Do I get to pick the time?"

"If you get on the stick! How did you let her get away from you?"

"I never had her." Lynn's tone was impatient. "She and I have never been anything but friends."

Vivian said tartly, "You could probably win her over if you'd forget your old movies and popcorn, and spend more time with moonlight and roses."

"I'm not the moonlight and roses type. Besides, I never wanted to trap Megan. I wanted her to fall in love with me — popcorn, old movies, and all." Lynn took a sip of her cappucino. "It seems a little late now, though. If you hadn't noticed, Megan and Randall are together."

"I think you could change that, if you wanted to."

"I'd like it to change, but I'm not interested in changing it. I love Megan. I'd like her to be happy. If Randall is what she wants, I hope it works out for her."

"Next you'll be telling me that you're not jealous."

"No, I won't." Lynn's voice betrayed a flash of the feelings she controlled so well. "I'm jealous as hell. I'm so jealous I'd die before I'd let her know. Because I'm a firm believer in the fact that those who grovel and beg get nothing but contempt."

The music changed and the four women returned to the table.

"Would you like to dance, Megan?" Lynn asked, not looking at Vivian.

"Yes, I would," Megan said.

When they reached the edge of the dance floor, Lynn extended her arms and Megan fitted herself inside them. As they came together, Lynn was very aware of the fullness of Megan's body against her own. Megan's perfume smelled clean and slightly sweet. Lynn took a deep breath as they started to move slowly across the dance floor.

"In all the years I've known you, I don't think I've ever danced with you like this," Megan remarked. "You're good."

"You say that about all the women you dance with," Lynn teased. "You said the same thing about Vivian."

"That's different. She's a good dancer, but you and I fit together. Can't you feel it?"

107

Lynn smiled. "I think I know what you mean. We do fit well."

Megan relaxed further and the fit was even better. She felt comfortable in Lynn's arms and didn't want the music to stop. When it did, she didn't back away. "Let's dance again."

The band began "I Had the Craziest Dream," and Lynn and Megan continued to dance. As they moved to the music, Megan said sadly, "Ellen and Joyce would have liked this place. Ellen would have loved the music." She looked at Lynn. "I miss both of them an awful lot at times."

"Me too." Lynn's voice was soft.

"You know, it helps just to know you understand. Just to know you shared that part of my life."

"I feel the same way about you." Lynn smiled into Megan's eyes. "We've been through a lot of history together."

"Lynn, how come you never mentioned Jill to me?" Megan asked.

"It just never came up. Besides, you've been pretty involved during the past few months."

"Are you in love with her?"

The music stopped and Lynn released Megan. For a moment the two of them stood there.

"Are you?" Megan's gray eyes were fastened on Lynn's.

"I'm not sure," Lynn lied. She began walking toward the table. "I guess time will have to answer that question."

The six women talked and danced until early morning. The rest of the week went by quickly. Although neither woman verbalized the fact, both Lynn and Megan were happy when the time came to return to Atlanta.

Chapter 26

The Friday evening had arrived for Megan to ask Randall for her decision. They had finished dinner and sat side by side. The sound and warmth of the fire filled the den.

"Randall?" Megan said. "Time's up. What are you going to do?"

Randall had bitten skin off her bottom lip. The month, she realized, had worked two ways. It had brought Megan into a deeper involvement with her, but it had also brought her into a deeper involvement with Megan.

She looked at Megan with tear-filled eyes that pleaded for her: "I need more time. I can't leave right now."

Megan closed her eyes. A scalpel on her nerve endings could not have caused more pain. She felt the warmth of her own tears. "There is no more time. That was our agreement."

"I love you, Megan. You're not going to hold me to that stupid agreement, are you? How could you just say good-bye to me? I thought you loved me."

"I do love you. That's one of the reasons we can't continue like this. I'm not interested in some clandestine affair. I want a relationship."

"Clandestine affair?" Randall's tone was a mixture of anger and defensiveness. "Gay life *is* a clandestine affair. How can you object to hiding from my husband, and then ask me to hide from the world?"

"Is that what you understand? That I object to hiding from your husband? I object to sharing you. Not just sexually, but sharing your commitment. God, Randall, there are so few things in life that people are really committed to! I want a relationship where I'm number one, where the commitment to each other is total. I offer that, and I want it in return. I *demand* it in return. I won't take less."

The heat of Megan's words brought color to her face. "I can't offer you social acceptance like your marriage to Kenneth provides. There is no legal ceremony to mark the commitment two gay people make to each other. But we do have the recognition and social acceptance of our friends — some gay, some straight."

Megan forced a smile. "In a way, Randall, a gay couple has to be stronger than a heterosexual couple. We have to love each other enough to put up with the world's hostility. The only thing that keeps us together is our loving. The only people on the planet who would get into such a relationship are two people who love each other very deeply, more deeply than the world in general has the power to understand. If you don't love me that deeply, then you don't love me enough."

Randall could no longer convert her guilt into anger. She was weeping quietly. "I don't love enough. I don't want to hide." She brushed the tears from her face. "I just can't live with the whole world thinking I'm some kind of . . . ." She took Megan's hand. "I love you, but I can't live like that."

Megan felt numb. She placed both her hands around Randall's. "I understand."

"I don't want to lose you. Why can't we go on like we have been?"

Megan's voice was very gentle. "I can't do that. I'd lose respect for myself if I did and I'd begin to hate you. If we trapped each other in that kind of affair, neither of us would have a chance at a complete relationship." Megan attempted a smile. "I really want that kind of relationship again. I know how wonderful it can be. I want someone I can have that kind of caring with again."

Randall wiped her cheeks and stared at Megan. Jealousy and anger replaced the guilt. "I'm sure Lynn Bradley would be happy to play house with you," she said sharply. "I've see how you look at her. You have more than a feeling of friendship for her. I don't know why you always deny it."

"Don't do this. Don't look for something to fight about. It won't make breaking up any easier." Megan's eyes were soft gray tenderness. "Lynn has nothing to do with you and me. We're not breaking up because of her, and you know that."

Megan paused for an instant, catching Randall's hand with her own. "Randall, I've asked you to leave your husband and live with me. If I committed myself to you, I would keep that commitment."

Randall's anger was gone. She squeezed Megan's hand. "If I get my act together, can I call you?"

"If you ever decide to leave Kenneth, give me a call."

"I guess I'd better go," Randall said.

Megan walked her to the door. Randall kissed her gently. They smiled at each other and stood for a moment holding hands.

"Are you sure we can't meet every now and then just to keep in practice?"

"I'm sure," Megan replied evenly.

"I won't forget you," Randall said softly.

"Nor I you," Megan said and closed the door. She leaned against it and wept.

Chapter 27

At one minute after midnight Lynn Bradley rang Megan's doorbell.

She brushed past Megan and walked to the den. "I had a late emergency out this way. I saw your light and decided to stop."

Lynn flopped down on one of the loveseats. "I arrived just in time to see Randall leave. I take it she isn't coming back tonight. I waited to see if you sent her to the store for something. When she didn't return in fifteen minutes, I decided to visit."

Megan smiled broadly at Lynn. "You're a nut, a certifiable nut."

"A few of my patients have told me the same thing. In my business it helps. But we call it being creative."

"Would you like something to drink?"

"Coffee would be nice."

They stacked a tray with coffee and cookies and returned to the den. The fire was still burning, and Megan added another log.

Megan managed a casual tone. "You were right, of course. She couldn't picture herself committed to a woman, not if it meant giving up her social respectability, among other things. It seems, as you so wisely pointed out, that sleeping with a woman is one thing, but leaving a husband and making a commitment to that woman is quite another. She never had any intention of leaving her husband."

Lynn leaned toward Megan. "I'm sorry, Meggie. But I'd honestly rather you know this now instead of six months from now."

"I know. I was stupid to get involved in the first place. If I could change it, I would."

Lynn was filled with tenderness for Megan. She wanted this woman's happiness as much as she wanted her own.

"Don't be too hard on yourself. In a way, it's good that it happened. Ellen had been gone for fourteen months, and apparently it would have taken the kind of attraction you felt for Randall to move you off dead center."

She paused briefly, then continued, "You deserve better than Randall. Ellen would want you to be happy. I want you to be happy."

"You know, it's funny, Lynn. You challenge my thoughts and beliefs more than anyone I know. You tell me the truth, even when I'd rather hear a lie." She smiled. "And despite that, I'm more comfortable with you than I am with any other person I know. I like it that you won't just give me polite conversation and platitudes. I don't always like hearing what you have to say, but I always respect it. And I always know you're telling me the truth."

Lynn smiled warmly. "I'll always be here for you, Meggie. However, at the moment you need some sleep."

"You know where the guest room is if you want to spend the night."

"I'll just head on home. I think you're doing okay, considering the circumstances. If you need me, call and I can be here in ten minutes."

Chapter 28

For the next six weeks Megan again tried consciously to lose herself in her work. She applied for and immediately received a grant to assist in research to improve an artificial heart prototype to be used as an intermediate step when a human heart was not available for transplant. The research was extremely interesting, and she found herself thinking less and less about Randall.

Lynn kept her busy in most of her off-duty hours. They ate dinner together at least three times a week and watched old movies on cassettes or on the Movie Classics channel. Megan had begun to laugh more, to look forward to the time she spent with Lynn.

Lynn, even more in love with Megan, was determined that if they would ever be more than friends, it would be because

Megan wanted it as much as she. For the present, she felt content to share as much time as they did together.

The phone awakened Megan at eight o'clock on a Sunday morning.

"Hi. I need to talk to you. Can I come over there?"

"Is something wrong? Where are you?" Megan, jarred into wakefulness, was surprised to hear Randall's voice.

"I'm about ten minutes from your house. I really need to see you, Megan. I'm leaving Kenneth."

Megan felt her heart begin to race.

"Megan, are you there? Can I come over?"

"Yes, of course. Come right away."

Megan took a quick shower and had just finished dressing when the doorbell rang.

"Can I get you anything?" Megan asked as they sat opposite each other in the den. Megan looked directly into Randall's eyes. They were even bluer than she had remembered.

"I've missed you terribly. I want us to be together," Randall said, her voice soft and pleading.

"You said you were leaving Kenneth. When?" Megan's eyes were glued on Randall.

"I started seeing a psychiatrist three weeks ago. It may take three or four weeks, but I *am* leaving. I've done a lot of thinking, and I believe I can get past my need for society's approval."

Randall got up and sat down next to Megan. "Please don't make me wait any longer. I want us to be together again. If I didn't, I wouldn't be in therapy." She reached to Megan, held Megan's face between her hands. "You have to know I love you. If I feel it this much, you have to feel it too."

Megan took Randall's hands into her own. "I do feel your love for me, but are you sure you want to leave Kenneth?"

"I don't believe you! I came here to give you my good news, and you want to talk me out of it." Randall grinned and put her arms around Megan and pulled her closer. "I love you, lady. I want to spend my life with you."

Megan felt real hope again. She could feel the beat of her own heart. She looked at Randall with immense tenderness. "I've missed you. I'm glad you're back." She kissed Randall gently. "I love you."

Randall placed Megan's hand on her breast and kissed her full on the mouth. "I want to make love with you. Now."

When the doorbell rang two hours later, Megan sat bolt upright in bed.

"Oh, God! I forgot about Lynn. I was supposed to go to lunch with her!" Megan got up, grabbed a bathrobe and ran to the stairs.

"I thought we were going to lunch," Lynn said before her mind registered Megan's robe.

"Come on in." Megan could feel her warm face and knew she was blushing.

"Isn't that Randall's car out there?" Lynn felt the jealously and anger rise within her.

"Yes, she's upstairs."

Lynn was silent.

"She's been seeing a psychiatrist for several weeks. She plans to leave Kenneth," Megan tried to explain.

"When? Today?" Lynn's eyes were like glass. The mint green color had turned dark with controlled anger.

"That's what she's in therapy for." Megan was defensive, annoyed by the question. "Maybe as soon as three or four weeks. You're a psychiatrist. How long do things like that usually take?"

"Megan, I can't be your psychiatrist," Lynn snapped. "If you really want an answer, ask Randall's psychiatrist."

"I hope I'm not interrupting anything," Randall said, walking into the room wearing one of Megan's robes. "If you'll wait a few minutes, Lynn, Megan and I will get dressed and go to lunch with you. I'm starved."

I bet you are, Lynn thought. Her anger was plummeting into despair. "Thanks anyway," she said quickly. "I'm afraid I'll have to grab a quick sandwich. I have to run by the hospital."

"How about later? Can you come to dinner? You can celebrate our reunion with us," Randall offered.

"Sorry, but I have a date," Lynn replied with a forced smile. She moved toward the door. Turning to Megan, she said, "Give me a call next week if you have time."

Chapter 29

"I love that movie more every time I see it," Randall said as Megan clicked off the VCR. "I almost know the dialogue by heart."

"Well, here's looking at you, kid." Megan lifted her coffee cup in a toast.

"Does that mean you want more amaretto coffee before I leave?" Randall leaned over and kissed Megan on the cheek.

"What time do you have to go?" Megan set her cup on the table.

"Not for another thirty or forty minutes."

Megan put her arm around Randall's shoulders and pulled her closer. "I like holding you."

"And I like being held." Randall nestled her head against Megan's breasts.

For a full minute neither spoke. Megan had been particularly happy during the past six weeks. She had so thoroughly accepted Randall's spoken intention to leave Kenneth that in all that time she had not mentioned his name once. She had grown used to Randall's presence, to the two or three evenings each week Randall spent with her. Megan was aware of the passage of time but had promised herself that she would be patient.

"I almost forgot, Randall said. "I have to be in New York Monday and Tuesday of next week." She tilted her head and smiled up at Megan." I volunteered so I can get a long weekend with you next week."

"You mean a spend-the-night type weekend?" Megan asked eagerly.

"Yes, Kenneth will be out of town for a week."

"Do you think you can change your appointment with your psychiatrist? I'll get someone to cover for me, we can go out of town too."

"Sounds good," Randall said. "My appointment's no problem. I've been meaning to tell you, I'm not seeing Dr. Waters any more."

"So who are you seeing?"

"No one. I think it was a waste of time and money. After an entire month I couldn't tell one bit of difference."

Megan sat up straight. "You stopped seeing the psychiatrist *five weeks ago?*"

"Yes, I'm sorry I didn't mention it, but it didn't seem important."

Megan could feel the jolt of adrenalin move through her body as the meaning of Randall's words became clear. "You stopped seeing the psychiatrist one week after we started seeing each other again?" Megan was glaring at Randall. "I thought he was going to help you leave Kenneth."

121

"That was the idea when I started, but after I saw how well you and I were getting along, I knew I could leave on my own." Randall smiled. "It's just a matter of timing."

"Timing?" Megan was furious. "What kind of timing?"

"What are you so angry about? Nothing's changed. I still intend to leave Kenneth."

"Really, Randall?" Megan's voice was strained. "What's stopping you?"

"I want to get some of our finances straightened out, so Kenneth doesn't take me to the cleaners."

"Money! Money is stopping you?" Megan stood up so quickly she knocked the empty coffee cup to the floor. The sound of shattering china distracted her momentarily; she watched Randall bend down to pick up the pieces.

"Leave it," Megan said in a quiet voice. "I'll clean it up later."

"Megan, please listen." Randall sat back and looked up at Megan. "I love you. I intend to live with you. I just need more time."

"I'm afraid you'll always need more time." Megan's anger had transformed into hurt and helplessness. "You should have told me about the psychiatrist. I had a right to know. I had such hope for what would come out of those sessions." Her eyes spoke to Randall's. "They gave me hope. Now you tell me it's money that keeps you with Kenneth. You're a bright woman, Randall. You could earn a good living for yourself. Even if you couldn't, don't you think that I have enough money to take care of us?"

Randall's face hardened. "I'm not willing to let Kenneth walk away with property and money that I've worked for. If you'll give me more time, I won't have to hand everything over to him."

"You take whatever time you need." Megan's voice was even. "When you leave Kenneth, call me."

Randall looked at her, aghast. "You don't want to see me until then?"

"It's not a matter of wanting or not wanting to see you. If I go on like this, hoping one minute, and no hope the next, it will eventually affect my feeling for you, my work, my entire life. I can't have that."

Randall looked at her watch. "Megan, can't we talk about this tomorrow? I have to leave now." She stood up.

"It wouldn't change anything," Megan said firmly. "Please, Randall, don't call me until you've left Kenneth for good."

"Do you really mean that?" She glanced again at her watch.

"I really mean it."

Randall moved to Megan and kissed her. "You'll hear from me soon."

Chapter 30

Lynn and Megan had managed to get a secluded corner table in the hospital cafeteria. Lynn listened attentively as Megan told her what had happened between her and Randall.

"I'm really sorry, Maggie. I know this whole thing has been awfully painful for you." Lynn's voice was quiet and kind. "Are you serious about getting back together with her?"

"I'd try again if she left Kenneth," Megan said wearily, "but I'm not holding my breath. I have a feeling that I'd be navy blue before it happens."

"Maybe not. Randall may surprise you."

"Maybe." Megan smiled. "How about you and Jill letting me take you to dinner tonight?"

"That would be nice," Lynn said as she took a sip of iced tea. "But Jill and I are no longer dating. She's seeing someone else."

Megan was suddenly aware that she felt better. "In that case I'll take you to dinner."

That dinner was the first of many. Lynn and Megan fell easily into old patterns of friendship. To those old patterns, they added a new dimension. They went dancing once a week at a new club that offered a change from disco and rock, playing the current love songs, mixed with hits of the 70s and 80s. Fast numbers were sprinkled in occasionally, but the majority of the music was slow and romantic. Dancing was close and relaxed.

Megan's feelings for Lynn had changed considerably. When she looked at her these days, she saw more than a good friend — she saw a very attractive and sexy woman. On more than one occasion she was seriously tempted to invite Lynn to spend the night. What stopped her was the lingering hope that one day Randall would leave Kenneth. She knew that a relationship with Lynn would end the moment Randall called, that Lynn would be devastated. Megan cared too much for Lynn to take the chance that she would inflict such pain on her closest and most beloved friend.

Megan found the time before Christmas particularly busy. She didn't get to spend much time with Lynn, and to her surprise, she missed her. Lynn had accepted an appointment to a faculty position at Emory University School of Medicine, and she was teaching a class in emergency psychiatric care to third- and fourth-year students. The class met three times a week and demanded much of Lynn's free time.

Megan spent the last two weeks in November and the first week in December in Boston, learning a promising new surgical technique for open heart surgery. She worked daily in the cardiac care unit with its chief resident, Janet Marko, a bright, pretty thirty-year-old. Suspecting that their rapport had more than a professional basis, Megan accepted an invitation to her home for dinner. But the two women discussed only surgical procedures before, during, and after dinner.

On Megan's second visit to Janet's home, the two women sat in front of the fire drinking coffee after dinner.

"You're a very good cook," Megan complimented her again.

"I enjoy cooking," Janet answered. "It's one of the ways I like to relax. Do you cook?"

Megan chuckled. "Afraid not. I have no talent and very little interest in the culinary arts." She added with a smile, "Although, as you have seen, I do like to eat."

"Does your roommate cook?" Janet asked casually.

"I don't have a roommate. I use delivery services a lot."

"Are you divorced?" Janet inquired.

"No, I'm single. Why do you ask?" Megan had a good idea where Janet was heading, but she decided it would be wiser to let Janet broach the subject.

"You're a very attractive woman. It seems unlikely that you wouldn't be involved with someone. I guess I'm curious." Janet smiled disarmingly.

Megan put her cup on the table beside her chair and looked directly at her. "Janet, if there's something you want to ask me, why don't you just throw caution to the wind and ask me outright?"

"I guess I wasn't as subtle as I'd hoped to be," Janet said with a smile. "My intuition tells me that you're gay. Are you?"

Amused, Megan fenced with her. "Do you ask all of your dinner guests that question, or am I an exception? Why do you want to know?"

"You're the first dinner guest I've had in about two months, and no, I don't ask because I usually know before I invite someone to dinner." Janet met Megan's eyes dead on. "I want to know because I like you very much, and I'm very attracted to you. Actually, I'd like to go to bed with you."

"Well, you're certainly direct!" Disconcerted, Megan leaned back in her chair. She looked at the young woman before her. Janet was intelligent, attractive, desirable.

"I find you very attractive, too," Megan confessed with a sigh, "but I have no intention of going to bed with you. At least not right now."

"May I ask why not? Are you involved with someone?"

"Not in the sense of a formal or even an informal commitment. There *is* someone I care about very much and I'm not sure exactly what will come of it. Until I know for sure it wouldn't be fair to anyone else to start something. I'm not good at casual sex, Janet. I have a way of becoming emotionally involved with someone I sleep with."

"And if I tell you that I'd like to get to know you, that I'm not looking for a one-night stand, would that make any difference?"

Megan gazed at the lithe, shapely body, then into the intelligent brown eyes. "You don't make it easy, Janet."

"I guess I find it hard to take no for an answer," Janet said softly. "I'm used to getting what I want."

"If it's any consolation . . ." Megan leaned forward. "You're a very attractive woman."

"But the answer is still no?"

"The answer is still no. With the added comment that if things were different in my life, my answer could be very different."

"Your friend is a very lucky woman. If it doesn't work out for you two, I'd like the chance to get better acquainted."

127

* * * * *

On Megan's return, as she was walking through the airport gate, she spotted Lynn. "It's good to see you," Megan said, hugging Lynn a little more tightly than usual. "I missed you."

Lynn hugged back. "That's the best news I've had in three weeks." She added reproachfully, "I was sure you'd forgotten me when you left me alone on Thanksgiving Day."

"I'm sorry the schedule worked out like that, but I did call. And in just a couple of weeks we'll be in Aspen skiing our hearts out."

"Did you bring me a present from Boston?" Lynn teased.

"Present? What happened to the woman who was satisfied with my company?"

"No present," Lynn said, with a sigh. "I hope your company isn't all I'm getting for Christmas."

"Only good children get Christmas presents. You'll more than likely get coal in your stocking."

"And have you been good, Dr. McKenzie?" Lynn smiled.

"I've been very, very good. In fact, you wouldn't believe just how good I've been."

"That sounds as though you had the opportunity to be naughty." Lynn looked at her with alert interest.

"I wouldn't call it an opportunity. Just an offer."

"You didn't accept?" Lynn felt more than a tinge of jealousy.

"No, I didn't. I'm not rushing into anything ever again."

"Good girl." Lynn smiled approval.

"How about me taking you to dinner tonight?"

"I already have a dinner date with one of the members of my department at Emory. She has an interesting idea for an article, she's asked me to co-author it with her. We're going over some ideas tonight."

"What time do you have to be there? Maybe you can stop by for a drink after you're finished."

Lynn glanced at her watch. "I have just enough time to drop you off at the house and get to her place by seven. It may be ten or ten-thirty before we're finished. Would that be too late for me to come by?"

Megan realized how much she had missed Lynn; she was eager for her company. "Come by, no matter what time it is. I was looking forward to being with you this evening."

"If you'd let me know sooner when you were getting back, I wouldn't have accepted the invitation. I can't change it," Lynn said regretfully. "Ruth is leaving town the day after tomorrow. She'll be gone four weeks, and I need to hear her ideas on the article before she leaves."

"Just come by when you're finished." Megan smiled at Lynn. "I've really missed you."

Chapter 31

Dr. Ruth Evans had been on the faculty at Emory Medical School for a year, having moved to Atlanta from Maine. The breakup of her five-year relationship had not come as a complete surprise; Ruth had known for years that she and her lover had serious problems in their relationship. She sold her house and furniture, moved to Atlanta, and started over. The starting over did not include dating at first, but gradually she began to meet people.

She had heard about Lynn through mutual friends but had not met her until Lynn began teaching at Emory. Because each knew the other was gay and had heard much about each other, including that they really should meet, their friendship had gotten off to a running start.

The two talked about medicine and psychiatry and discussed mutual friends over dinner. Ruth Evans was an expert on wines and served several excellent vintages during dinner. When the meal was finished, they moved to the den.

"You'll love this Bordeaux. It's very dry and full-bodied," Ruth said as she handed Lynn her fourth glass for the evening.

"If I have much more of your wonderful wines, I won't be any good tonight as a co-author," Lynn protested.

"It helps to get the creative juices flowing," Ruth replied. "What we need is a little music to help it along." She turned on the cassette deck that already held six cassettes she had carefully selected earlier.

"Too bad I'm leaving town so soon," Ruth said as she sat down next to Lynn. "We could spend the time working on the paper."

"I'm afraid that wouldn't work out even if you weren't leaving town. I'm leaving for Aspen in a couple of weeks and I'll be pretty busy till then."

"I haven't been to Aspen in years. Are you going alone?"

"With a friend. She owns a lodge there." Lynn looked at her watch. "In fact, I promised her I'd stop by on the way home. We better get to work before I'm too high to contribute anything."

"Don't be silly. Wine relaxes more than it intoxicates." Ruth took a swallow from her glass. "I love Barbra Streisand." She took Lynn's hand. "Come on, Lynn, dance with me."

Lynn put her glass down. As they moved together, Ruth held her body inch for inch next to Lynn's. The room was slightly warm, and the heat added to Lynn's mounting intoxication.

Ruth ran her fingers along the back of Lynn's neck. "You're a very attractive woman," she murmured.

The song ended, and they sat back down. Ruth filled Lynn's glass again. "Come on, have one more glass of wine and we'll get started on that paper."

"I've already had more than I should," Lynn protested. But she took a sip from her glass.

"I think you have an eyelash under your eye. Let me get it." Ruth leaned toward Lynn and lightly touched her face. "Close your eyes a minute."

The room spun slightly as Lynn complied. Ruth leaned closer and kissed Lynn on the lips. She kissed her again, moving her hand to Lynn's breast.

Lynn felt warm and lightheaded. Without consent her body moved to respond to Ruth's touch. Her lips parted as Ruth kissed her again, and desire claimed a life of its own. The soft tongue moved inside her mouth, sending pleasant sensations washing over her. She drew her breath in sharply as a hand slid between her legs and rested there, sending its warmth directly into her. Lynn's hands moved automatically to the back of Ruth's neck. They moved in light, delicate paths along the fine skin and into Ruth's soft hair.

"Let's go upstairs," Ruth murmured, her mouth caressing Lynn's.

"I'm not sure I . . ." Her words were silenced by the insistent strokes of Ruth's tongue. Hands moved to her blouse and began undoing the buttons. Lynn's breathing was rapid as her own desire took control. She quivered as the soft hands moved to her skin and caressed her bare breasts.

She pulled her mouth from Ruth's. "I think I'd better go." Her hands covered Ruth's and stopped them.

"You don't want to leave, Lynn." The dark eyes were hypnotic. "Look at yourself. It's been a long time, hasn't it?" She kissed her lips lightly. "I want to make love with you, and you want it too."

Ruth's hands pulled free of Lynn's grasp without resistance. Her hands massaged the softness of Lynn's breasts and raised the creamy flesh to meet her engulfing mouth.

Lynn's desire moved well beyond her control. Electric sensations claimed her body and shocked her passion into flames.

"Where's your bedroom?" Lynn heard her voice from a distance as she moved her hands inside Ruth's blouse and kneaded the full breasts.

They climbed the stairs like Siamese twins, clinging to each other. Ruth hit the light switch as they entered her bedroom.

"Do you mind if I leave the light on?"

"I like the light." Lynn pushed her mouth hungrily against Ruth's.

They undressed each other without patience, clothes falling around them at random.

"Do you always go to dinner without underwear?" Ruth said.

Lynn bent to kiss Ruth's breasts. "Frequently. I don't like to feel restricted."

"There are no restrictions here.'" Ruth raised Lynn's face, brought her lips to hers, and slid her tongue into her mouth.

The dark burgundy satin sheets felt cool against Lynn's fevered skin. She lay crosswise on the king-sized bed as Ruth knelt between her legs. Insistent hands spread her legs further apart. Then the warm mouth was moving on her, stroking the satin softness of her lips, the tongue sensually stroking her. Fingers entered her and a shock of pleasure moved through her body. Her mind was overrun with images, all soft, insistent, and hot. Her hips moved slowly at first, increasing their speed as pleasure grew more intense. Convulsive movements racked her body as pleasure burst and ecstasy filled her. Her cry was low and steady as she felt herself rise on the crest of pleasure, suspended in space, floating in a world of ultimate sensation.

Hands trailed along her body as Ruth lay next to her, placing small kisses on her ear and cheek; Ruth's warm breath moved against her hair and skin.

"I thought you'd be like this," Ruth murmured. "All fire and heat beneath the professional exterior. Your patients would be shocked."

"I don't sleep with my patients." Lynn looked into the dark brown eyes. Her hands moved to the softness between Ruth's legs. She stroked gently, dipping her fingers into Ruth, spreading the wetness along the satin folds. She watched the pleasure and desire in Ruth's face in response to her caresses. Her mouth traveled leisurely down Ruth's body, licking and kissing. She trailed her tongue against the soft inner thighs, the tip moving upward. It darted, stroked, and caressed. It moved gently, firmly, roughly along and between the silken folds and moved to concentrate on the tiny jewel of firmness. Her fingers entered Ruth and added their motion to the pleasure coursing through Ruth's body. Pleasures merged, Ruth made a loud, deep moaning sound, and her body shook with ecstasy. Then Ruth's body fell silent and still against the sheets, her hands limp at her sides. Lynn's mouth nuzzled her gently for a moment, moved upward to caress her lips with a feather's kiss.

They lay side by side, Lynn's head on Ruth's shoulder, an arm and a leg lying lightly across her body.

"Now aren't you glad you stayed?" Ruth asked, turning toward Lynn.

Lynn's eyes were closed. Ruth sat up slightly, reached for the sheet at the foot of the bed, and pulled the silkiness over them. Her hand returned to Lynn's soft hair and face.

"I'm glad you stayed," Ruth whispered. Her eyes closed, and she joined Lynn in sleep.

Chapter 32

When Lynn returned home the next morning, she found a note taped to the front door: *Please call me at the office to let me know you're all right. Megan.*

Lynn put the note on the hall table, went upstairs and took a shower. Dressed, she sat on the edge of the bed and dialed Megan's office. Megan was in surgery and would not be free until one o'clock. Lynn left word that she would stop by Megan's house about seven.

Lynn's first patient was at ten, and she stayed busy until five. The day passed quickly. Before going to Megan's she stopped at home and changed into jeans and a sweater.

Megan flung open the door as Lynn was about to ring the bell. "Where the hell were you last night?" She demanded before Lynn was through the doorway.

"I'm sorry I didn't call you. I should have. The time just got away from me."

They went into the den. Her hands on the hips of her red jogging pants, Megan stood over Lynn, bristling. "You've never done this before. What the hell happened? I was worried sick. I didn't know whether you'd been in an accident or just received a better offer. I didn't know your friend's name, so I couldn't call. . . ." Megan began to pace.

"At twelve-thirty last night I was sitting outside your house. Then I decided I had to get some sleep so I'd be awake for surgery this morning. It was one-thirty when I left the note. I telephoned at five-thirty before I left for the hospital, and you *still* weren't home. Where the hell *were* you?"

"Megan, I'm sorry you were worried. I should have called. I didn't plan to be out all night."

"Where *were* you?"

"I told you I was going to dinner at a faculty member's home. And that's where I was." Lynn was starting to feel irked. "I should have called you. I'm sorry."

"Did you spend the night with this faculty member?" Megan could feel the blood pounding in her temples.

"Megan, why are you so angry?" Lynn's own anger was mounting.

"Answer me. Did you spend the night with that woman? Did you sleep with her?"

"Since when has my sex life been any of your business?"

"Damn it, Lynn," Megan shouted, "you did sleep with her, didn't you?" Her face was almost purple.

"Yes, I slept with her," Lynn yelled back. "Is that what you wanted to hear? I slept with her. We made love. Why are you so damn angry? You and I are not lovers. We're friends. I don't have to ask your permission to sleep with someone."

Megan sat down and put her face in her hands. "I thought I knew you better. I didn't think you were the type to jump into bed with people you just met." She glared at Lynn. "Boy, was I ever wrong."

Lynn sat opposite Megan and looked directly at her. "I don't jump into bed with people I've just met, and you know it. I haven't made love with anyone in more than two years."

"Until last night," Megan sneered.

"Until last night," Lynn quietly confirmed.

"Did you seduce her, or was it her idea?"

"Megan, stop this. You don't know what you're saying." Lynn wanted to keep her own anger from escalating.

"What made her so special? Are you in love with her?" Again Megan's face had become scarlet.

"It wasn't her. It just happened." Lynn sighed. "I had a lot to drink. Ruth came on to me and I responded. It was a combination of things." Lynn reached out for Megan's hand. "Megan, it just happened."

Megan pulled her hand away. "You haven't answered me. Are you in love with her?"

"No, I'm not in love with her. I don't even know her that well. It was a purely physical thing."

Megan jumped up and began to pace again. "I can't believe this. I can't believe I was worried sick about you — that I was sitting in front of your house while you were in bed with someone you don't even know."

"Now wait a minute, Megan." Lynn's patience was exhausted. "I've known her since I started to teach at Emory. It's not like I picked her up on the expressway."

"Do you intend to sleep with her again?"

"I hadn't really thought about it. I didn't plan to sleep with her last night."

"So you might sleep with her again?" Megan's wrath was again on the rise.

"Whatever I do with her isn't any of your business. Your sex life is your business, and mine is mine."

"So you don't care who I sleep with? Is that it?"

"Of course I care. You know that. But I don't have any right to tell you that you can't sleep with someone. I knew Randall was bad news, but I didn't tell you not to sleep with her. I repeat: you and I are not lovers."

Megan was running on raw, unreasoning emotion. "It's a good thing. I couldn't live with a bed hopper."

Lynn laughed. "Bed hopper! I've been to bed with one person, one time, in two years, and I'm a bed hopper? Come on, Megan, give me a break!"

"It sounds like Ruth what's-her-name is giving you all the breaks you need."

"Okay, I give up." Lynn threw her hands in the air. "Where do we go from here? Can we agree to disagree?"

"I'm not sure. I need to think about it."

"I don't understand, Megan," Lynn said in a calm voice. "You've pursued a sex life and a love life that didn't include me, and now you expect me to answer to you for *my* choices? It doesn't work that way. You don't get to run your life and my life too. Friends don't have that much say in each other's lives."

Megan looked away. "At this point I'm not even sure I want to be friends."

"You're being ridiculous," Lynn said, putting her hands on Megan's shoulders. She spoke in a quiet voice.

"You shouldn't have gone to bed with Ruth," Megan said as she pulled away. "I don't think we should spend as much time together anymore."

"You're not serious!" Lynn felt crushed.

"I'm serious. You found someone you're interested in. I need to find someone, too. I can't do that if we're always together. So after tonight, I don't plan to see you as often."

It was the final straw. "There's an old saying, Megan: Be careful what you pray for; you may get it." Her voice had become steel. "If distance is what you want between us, you've got it. Starting now."

Lynn walked toward the door.

"Are you leaving?" Megan asked, suddenly uncertain about what was happening between them.

Lynn turned and looked at her. "Do you want me to stay?"

Jealously again gained the upper hand. "No, I really don't care where you go."

Lynn was too angry to speak. She turned and stalked to the door.

"Go, spend the night with Ruth, for all I care," Megan shouted after her. "I don't care what you do."

The door slammed.

Chapter 33

That night Ruth Evans telephoned Lynn. She was leaving the following afternoon, she wanted to talk to Lynn before she left. Lynn reluctantly agreed to stop by her home.

"Can I fix you a drink?" Ruth, trim and elegant in a long silk Chinese robe, sat cross-legged on the sofa in the den.

"No, thanks," Lynn said, thinking ruefully of the role drinking had played the night before.

"I want you to know that I really enjoyed last night." Ruth smiled. "I'd like to get to know you better. Hopefully last night won't be a one-time event."

"I'd be lying if I didn't say I enjoyed the evening immensely." Lynn forced an answering smile that was gone as quickly as it appeared. "I'd also be less than honest if I didn't tell you I don't think it will happen again. I'm not blaming the wine, but a number of things came together to create the circumstances between us. I'm flattered by your interest in me." This time Lynn's smile was less forced. "It's been a long time since I've spent an evening with someone who wanted me that much and let me know it. It was very easy to respond in kind."

"Why do I feel that the other shoe is about to drop?" Ruth asked wryly.

Lynn said slowly, carefully, "It's not that I don't find you attractive — last night speaks for itself. It's just that . . . there are things in my life right now that I need to sort out. Until that happens I really have no business starting a relationship with anyone."

"I can wait." Ruth shrugged her silk-clad shoulders. "If I had to guess, I'd say you had a run-in with your Aspen friend. You mentioned last night that you were supposed to drop by her place on the way home. I imagine she wasn't too happy when you didn't show up. I'd have been furious."

"I should have called her," Lynn admitted.

"As I remember, phone calls weren't on either of our minds last night."

Lynn smiled ruefully, "I wish it had crossed mine."

"You can't put the toothpaste back in the tube." Ruth leaned forward and kissed Lynn lightly on the lips. "I'd still like to get to know you better." She wrote a phone number on a piece of paper and handed it to Lynn. "This is where I'll be in New York for the next four weeks. If you don't go to Aspen, call and I'll meet you at the airport." She smiled seductively. "I can guarantee you a very nice Christmas in New York."

"I'll keep that in mind." Lynn put the paper in her pocket. "Thanks for understanding. Wish me luck."

Ruth laughed. "I'm not quite that much of a good sport."

141

Chapter 34

Kenneth Grayson had been pacing for an hour when he heard Randall's car pull into the garage. Moments later Randall walked into the den.

A desk lamp and the fire gave the only light to the room. A faint hit of pipe tobacco hung in the air, sweet and smelling of dark ripe cherries. Kenneth, in a maroon smoking jacket, was standing in front of the fire. He gestured toward a large winged-back chair in front of him. "Come, sit down. I want to talk with you."

Randall seated herself in the chair. Crossing her legs and running a tidying hand over her expensive gabardine pants, she looked at Kenneth. His tone made her uneasy.

"Where have you been?"

"I went to see a movie with Pat. I told you I was going out. Did you forget?"

"What did you see?" Kenneth's questions were sharp and precise — the kind he addressed to a witness on the stand for cross-examination.

Randall was ready for the question. "We went to the Classic Cinema and saw two Bogart films. Why?"

"Are you sure you went to a movie?" Kenneth's face was turning red.

"I don't have the best memory in the world, but I do remember where I was an hour ago. I was at the Classic Cinema with Pat." She looked more closely at Kenneth. "What's the matter with you?"

The veins in Kenneth's temples were standing out as he struggled for the self-control on which he so prided himself. "That's exactly what I was going to ask you. You've been home two evenings in the past three weeks. You were home exactly twice in the month before that."

"Are you keeping count, Kenneth?" Randall's tone had a slight edge.

Kenneth's eyes narrowed. He leaned over her and fastened his eyes on her face. "I'll tell you what I'm doing. I'm wondering where you spend so much time and with whom. I'm also beginning to think that the with whom is not another man, but a woman."

"Don't be ridiculous. I'm not involved with anyone, least of all a woman." Randall's voice was calm and appropriately amused.

"Is that so? Well, I happen to think differently. I've been adding a few things up, and you spend an awful lot of time with Pat Martin." He pulled a chair in front of Randall's and sat down. "I've also given some thought to the past, and I'd be willing to bet you were more than friends with that Dr. McKenzie." He leaned back in his chair. "I did a little checking at the office and I discovered that you *asked* to be relieved of McKenzie's account. You dragged around for more than a month afterward." He leaned forward again. "Is she the one who got you started, Randall? Did she drop you?"

"This is ridiculous!" Randall was indignant.

"I wish it were." Kenneth's voice was slow and deliberate. "If anyone had told me a year ago that my wife would be involved with a bulldyke, I'd have laughed in his face." His pupils were large black dots. "It's not so funny now."

"I'm sure Pat and Paul would be happy to know that you consider Pat a bulldyke," Randall said acidly. "As for Dr. McKenzie, if you'd ever seen her, you'd know she is no such thing."

"Tell me something else." Kenneth was closing in with his second revelation, satisfied that he had Randall off balance. "Did you plan to tell me about the baby, or did you think it too unimportant to mention?"

She gaped at him. "What do you mean?"

"Don't play games with me, Randall." Kenneth's eyes were daggers, and his voice was hot with anger. "Dr. Dunbar's office called to confirm the fact that you're pregnant. They wanted to know if you still plan to have an abortion."

He glared at her. "Tell me about my baby, Randall, the baby you're planning to get rid of."

"I was going to surprise you about the baby," she said, trying to regroup. "I'm sorry Dr. Dunbar ruined the surprise."

He leaned over her, his fists on his hips. "Were you going to surprise me with the abortion, too?"

"I hadn't fully decided on an abortion," she soothed him. "Since you talked to his office, you know that."

"Do you plan to carry the baby to term?" Kenneth's question was simple and direct; his eyes held hope.

"I'm not sure. It would change our lifestyle completely, and I'm not sure I want that."

"You mean you wouldn't be able to run around so easily?"
He didn't wait for a response. "Well, hear this. Either you carry
my baby to term, or I'll involve your ex-lover in a scandal that
will ruin her career and her life."

"Which alleged ex-lover are you talking about?"

Kenneth grabbed Randall's arm. "Don't play games with
me. You know damn well I'm talking about Dr. McKenzie." He
squeezed his fingers into her flesh. "I'm not kidding when I say
I'll ruin her."

"Does that go for Pat Martin, too?" Randall asked
sarcastically.

"I'll leave Pat Martin to her husband. Once I tell Paul what
you two are into, he'll take care of Pat without any help from
me."

"You have it all figured out, don't you? Well, see what you
can do with this." Randall's eyes were narrow flames. "There
is nothing you can do to make me have this baby. If I want an
abortion, you can't stop me. And an abortion is looking better
every minute."

Uncontrolled fury pulled Kenneth's muscles taut and sent
blood pounding against his veins and arteries. "What I can do,
and will do, unless you agree to have this baby, is to sue Dr.
McKenzie for alienation of affection."

Randall looked at him, stunned. "You wouldn't dare. You
have no case. And even if you did, where is your evidence? I
certainly won't testify for you." She leaned back, and her
words came more slowly. "Not to mention what the publicity
would do to you. You don't want that."

"You underestimate my feelings. I wouldn't like the
publicity but believe me, if it comes down to it, I'll take it in
order to get back at you." His face was dark with hate and
anger. "I'll drag your precious Dr. McKenzie through the courts
if I have to. I'll ruin both of you."

"Why her? What has she ever done to you?"

"You like her," he sneered. "Maybe even love her — as much as *you* can love anyone. That's reason enough. Something you want for something I want."

The fire shot sparks into the air as a log shifted with loud popping sounds. Randall sat unmoving. She looked straight ahead.

"You're out of your league here. I didn't get to be a senior partner in the firm because I'm tender hearted. I can size up a situation and reduce it to the bare essentials." He paused meaningfully. "The bare essential here can be stated very simply. You agree to have my child, and I'll forget about a suit against Dr. McKenzie. I'll give you tonight and tomorrow to think about it. If you haven't agreed by Friday, I'll file my suit. And as we both know, once I file the complaint, the news media will spread the story like jelly on bread."

For a moment neither spoke. The fire contributed the only sounds in the room. Kenneth watched Randall closely. *I have her*, he thought. *She can't win this one.* He had been in a battle of wills with Randall since the day they met. It was, admittedly, part of her attraction for him.

Randall met Kenneth's eyes. "What will you have if I agree? A child to raise? You don't really strike me as father material."

"I'll have a child to carry on my name. And we'll raise him together."

"Why not just divorce me and take the baby? If you really believe I'm sleeping with women, why would you want me?"

"Hell, I'd bet my last dime you had a fling with Dr. McKenzie and you're carrying on now with Pat Martin. It's not sharing you sexually in some schoolgirl game I object to, it's the time you're putting into your little charade. I want you here when you say you'll be here, that's all. If you can fit your women in on your own time, that's your business."

"What if *I* want a divorce?" Randall challenged him.

"And give up being Mrs. Kenneth Grayson? Sacrifice your social standing and your career with the firm? That doesn't sound like you." He held her eyes. "If you give me the baby and really want a divorce, I'll give it to you uncontested. But you leave with nothing. Not even your position with the firm."

"Why ever do you want us to stay together?" she asked incredulously.

"We're a perfect match. I understand you more than you think I do, and you are just beginning to understand me." He paused. "Besides, in my own way, I love you. I know what to expect from you. You don't keep me constantly off-guard with surprises."

Randall stood up. "I'm going to bed."

"Fine. I hope you sleep well. You have until Friday to make up your mind."

Chapter 35

Megan was astonished when the receptionist buzzed her to say that Randall Grayson was in the waiting room to see her.

"Show her in," Megan said, rising from behind her desk.

Randall walked quickly into the room.

"You're looking well. How have you been?" Megan asked as she took her hand. Randall's navy suit looked professional, but the lace ruffles of her blouse softened the look.

"Pretty good." Randall smiled. "I've missed you."

Randall sat in the same chair she'd taken the first time she had come to this office. "You look thinner. Have you lost weight?"

"A couple of pounds," Megan admitted. "It allows me a few guilt-free desserts." Her eyes caught Randall's and their light blue color enveloped her. "Were you just in the neighborhood? Or am I supposed to guess why you're here?"

Randall took a deep breath. "You're not going to like what I've come to tell you."

"Sounds ominous. What's wrong?"

"Kenneth is sort of on a rampage. He found out by accident that I'm pregnant."

"Are congratulations in order?" Megan kept her tone matter-of-fact.

"Not really. I'm not sure I want the baby. That's the root of Kenneth's anger. He intercepted a phone call from my doctor and learned not only that I'm pregnant but also that I'm considering an abortion." She paused. "He's furious. He really wants a child."

Megan was puzzled. "I don't mean to be rude, but what does all this have to do with me?"

"This is not easy to tell you, and it doesn't make a lot of sense unless you know how Kenneth thinks." Randall ran a smoothing hand over her skirt. "Kenneth has accused me of having affairs with you and with another woman friend, Pat Martin. He's threatened to tell Pat's husband."

Megan was more confused than ever.

Randall said slowly, "He's also threatened to sue you for alienation of affection."

"You're kidding!" Megan's eyes opened wide. "I hope you're kidding. Why in the world would he do such a thing?"

"He wants me to agree to have his baby." She met Megan's wide eyes. "If I'll have the baby, he's agreed to forget everything."

"How in God's name did I get into this?" Megan closed her eyes; her voice dropped to a whisper.

"He's sure I have feelings for you and that I wouldn't want you hurt."

149

"Can't you talk to him? You didn't admit to him that there was anything between us, did you?"

"Of course not," Randall said crisply. "But he's made up his mind. Either I agree by tomorrow to carry the baby to term, or he files suit."

"That's crazy! It will destroy your career and mine, and it won't do him any good either."

"I've seen him like this before. He'll cut his own throat to get what he wants."

"Do you plan to abort the baby?" Megan asked despairingly.

"I don't know — probably." Randall leaned forward. "I do have an idea for you."

"I could certainly use one." Megan sunk further into her chair.

"You need to contact an attorney and confront Kenneth as soon as possible. He knows he has no grounds, but at this point he wants to create havoc. If you confront him with the possibility of a countersuit, it might just shake him up enough to stop him."

"I'll contact someone right away. Are you sure you can't talk him out of this?"

"He wants the upper hand. He's not going to give an inch." She looked tenderly at Megan. "I'm so sorry you're involved in this. I insisted to Kenneth there was nothing between us. I really don't want you hurt."

Megan tried to conceal the rising tide of panic. "We're talking more than hurt here, Randall. A suit like that could ruin my career."

She looked at Randall and saw the sadness and love in her eyes. "I'll get an attorney right away. Thanks for warning me."

Randall smiled wistfully. "I can't live your life-style, but I really do love you." She stood up, walked to Megan, kissed her on the cheek. "I hope you never doubt that."

150

"I don't," Megan said without looking up.

"I'll be at my office if you need me." At the door, Randall turned again to Megan. "Having a baby is a serious step for me. I'd really hate it that Kenneth would have anything to do with the child's upbringing."

"I understand. I'm not asking you to have the baby to protect me," Megan said.

"Maybe you should ask me. I don't think I could say no to you."

"I care about you too much for that," Megan said.

"Thanks, Randall said. Her hand on the knob, she spoke again. "I wonder how long it will take you to figure out that you've been in love with Lynn all along."

Chapter 36

Megan telephoned Lynn's office and left word for her to come by her house as soon as possible. Lynn cancelled her last two appointments and was at Megan's house at four-thirty.

"What's wrong?" Lynn asked as Megan answered the door.

"You're not going to believe this one," Megan said as they walked to the den. She recounted her conversation with Randall.

Lynn shook her head in wonderment. "The man plays hard for what he wants. I've seen his kind before. They're very dangerous. I agree with Randall — you need to take the offensive. I know just the attorney to handle it. Margaret Bailey. I've been an expert witness several times when she was counsel. I've also known her personally for years. She's a brilliant woman, an outstanding trial lawyer. She and her husband have their own firm."

"She's straight?" Megan asked.

"Yes, but not homophobic. Do you want me to call her for you? We can at least find out what she advises."

Lynn reached Margaret Bailey at her home. With Megan joining in on an extension, Lynn explained the situation.

Margaret Bailey advised immediate confrontation with Kenneth Grayson. "I'll call him now and arrange a conference for first thing in the morning," she said with brisk authority.

Five minutes later Margaret called to confirm the meeting. "He'll see us at nine o'clock in his office. I want you to meet me at my office at eight-thirty."

"Do you mind if I come along?" Lynn inquired.

"I don't mind if Megan doesn't. In fact, a psychiatrist may add some clout. We are about to play a game of poker for very high stakes. See you two in the morning. Don't be late."

The morning air was cool with a promise of snow when Megan and Lynn picked up Margaret Bailey outside her office building. Margaret, in a severely tailored navy blue suit, was a striking woman, more imposing than physically attractive. Her short dark hair was laced with gray, the wire frames of her glasses matching its tone. She had eyes like a fox, deep brown, keenly aware, and ever vigilant.

The three women rode together to Kenneth Grayson's office, Margaret making notes as Megan answered herr sharply phrased questions.

"We're ready," Margaret said as Megan parked the car. "Just remember my instructions."

* * * * *

153

At exactly nine o'clock the three women were shown into Kenneth Grayson's office. Kenneth was alone, and he came forward to shake hands with Margaret, who introduced only herself. When everyone was seated, Margaret looked around the office in a three hundred and sixty degree sweep.

"I thought you had agreed to have your wife present. Did I misunderstand?"

"No, Randall is in her office and will join us as soon as I ask her to. I wanted a chance to meet with you first." He looked at Megan and then at Lynn. "Which of you is Dr. McKenzie?"

Margaret had instructed Megan and Lynn not to speak or answer questions unless she nodded her approval. She nodded toward Megan.

"I'm Dr. McKenzie." Megan met Kenneth's eyes dead on.

"And this," said Margaret Bailey, "is Dr. Lynn Bradley, a psychiatrist here in Atlanta."

"I've heard of Dr. Bradley." He looked at Lynn. "You have an excellent reputation as an expert witness."

Lynn nodded but did not speak.

Kenneth, standing, rested a hip on the edge of his desk. "What can I do for you and these ladies, Ms. Bailey?"

Margaret's speech was slow and deliberate. "My client, Dr. McKenzie, has been informed by your wife that you intend to place a civil suit against her for alienation of affection. Needless to say, this was, and is, very disturbing to Dr. McKenzie. Dr. McKenzie was shocked to receive such news, not only because of the sexual implications of such a charge, but even more, because your wife told her she had denied any sexual involvement with Dr. McKenzie. Ms. Grayson also mentioned that you had accused her of sexual involvement with a Patricia Martin. As I understand it, you, your wife, and Mr. and Mrs. Martin have known each other for years."

She raised an eyebrow slightly. "I don't pretend to understand the motivation for such accusations, and I'm not

154

here on Patricia Martin's behalf. However, I would be surprised if Ms. Martin didn't have an attorney here as soon as she learns of your statements concerning her and your wife."

Margaret crossed her arms; her smile was disconcertingly sudden. "Now I'm sure you can understand the damage that could be done to Dr. McKenzie's reputation by any such suit. The mere filing of such charges against a prominent cardiologist is sure to make the newspapers and the six o'clock news."

Margaret uncrossed her arms and leaned forward, her keen eyes boring into Kenneth. "Mr. Grayson, it would be a clear case of malicious slander, and we would be forced to file against you."

Kenneth sat tight-lipped, his own arms crossed. "Aren't you jumping the gun a little? Your client hasn't been served with any papers yet."

"That is exactly why we're here. As an attorney, I find this insanity — " Margaret cleared her throat. "Excuse me, may I have a glass of water?"

Kenneth poured water from the pitcher on his desk and handed it to Margaret. She drank about a third of it while everyone waited.

"Thank you. Where was I? Oh, yes. I find it difficult to believe that any intelligent attorney would bring such a suit without one witness or one shred of evidence."

She took another drink of water and smiled broadly at Kenneth. "By the way, I understand congratulations are in order. You must feel good about becoming a father." Her smile disappeared. "I am sorry to hear your wife is seeking an abortion against your wishes. That is bound to upset any man who is looking forward to fatherhood."

Kenneth's face turned deep red. "You seem very informed concerning my private life."

"We have Ms. Grayson to thank for that. Ms. Grayson made these statements in Dr. McKenzie's office yesterday. The transcript is being typed. I guess I forgot to mention that Dr. McKenzie's office has a voice-activated taping system she uses for case notes on patients' histories."

Margaret paused to let that piece of information sink in. "The reason your wife went to Dr. McKenzie's office is that she felt an injustice was about to be done to her. She wanted to warn Dr. McKenzie about your intended suit because she realized that you were making her a scapegoat for your marital problems. Ms. Grayson feels that you are trying to use her friendship with Dr. McKenzie as a bargaining chip to prevent her from obtaining an abortion."

Margaret finished the water. "That sounds to me — and I believe it would sound the same to a jury — like emotional terrorism, with Dr. McKenzie as the hostage. I would have to ask high monetary damages for intentional infliction of emotional distress."

She leaned forward and placed her empty glass on the edge of Kenneth's desk. "Not a pretty thought in any case. Particularly unbecoming to an officer of the court. Perhaps you can help me understand why you would threaten such an action against a woman you know to be innocent. A woman even your wife seeks to protect from what she describes as your terrible vindicative temper."

Kenneth Grayson unfolded his arms. His face was on the verge of purple. "I find it difficult to believe that my wife would have described me in that manner."

"Well, now." Margaret Bailey's voice moved in a slow drawl. "I heard that description myself. The tape is very clear. It's amazing what science can do these days."

Her eyes again bored into Kenneth. "Mr. Grayson, no rational person would carry this ridiculous business one step further. If you and your wife are having marital problems, wouldn't it be better to solve them out of the public eye? Lord knows, if my husband and I had gone to court with every problem and argument, neither of us would have a career in law today."

"This is all the result of a private misunderstanding that has gotten out of hand," Kenneth began. "Would you excuse me for a moment? I would like to speak to my wife."

"Certainly."

As the door closed, Margaret put her index finger across her lips in a silent warning to Megan and Lynn. She took a pen from her attache case, wrote a message on a piece of paper: "This office may have a recording device. Don't say anything. Just follow my lead and support whatever I say if I indicate to you that I want you to speak."

Margaret then spoke aloud for the benefit of any tape recorder that might be running, "I certainly hope Mr. Grayson rethinks any plans for a suit. However, I am a hundred percent sure that if he does proceed, we can easily prove malicious slander. It will do him and his wife a lot of damage, and the fool will be walking into it with his eyes wide open."

Kenneth burst into Randall's office and slammed the door. "Why the hell did you spill all our private business to Megan McKenzie?"

Randall looked up from her desk and threw her pen down. "Because I'm not willing to let you destroy an innocent person in your obsession to control me."

"I suppose you're going to tell me you were never involved with Pat Martin either?"

"Would you believe me if I did?" Randall's tone was acid.

"No, I wouldn't," Kenneth said.

157

"Then have it your way. Pat and I have been lovers for the past four months." Randall spat the words at Kenneth. "But I have never been involved with Megan McKenzie."

"So it's been Pat Martin all this time! I can't wait to see Paul's face when I tell him that his wife is my wife's lover."

"You don't want that, Kenneth. Paul would divorce Pat."

"I should think you two would want that. You could move in together. What a pair you'd make!"

"Kenneth, neither Pat nor I wants a divorce. If we had, we'd have asked for them. We're not lesbians. We were just experimenting, having a little fun. Neither of us wanted to leave our marriages." Randall laughed sarcastically. "You can't really think I'd want to live with a woman. You know me better than that. Do you think I'd throw my career away to live as a social outcast? Be reasonable, Kenneth. It's not as if I were cheating on you with another man."

Randall's thoughts were flying. She could only hope she was choosing the right words to diffuse Kenneth's anger. She was determined not to lose Pat as either a friend or a lover. No more declared, out-of-the-closet lesbians for her. They took their lives and their sexuality too seriously. Why not be married like everyone else, and then just have fun and enjoy the kind of sex you wanted without complications?

No more Megan McKenzies for her. The woman had reached her emotionally as well as physically. But being in love wasn't all there was in life. It didn't run the world. Status and social standing were important if one wanted to get ahead, and she couldn't have either with Megan. She wanted uncomplicated, friendly sex from now on — sex that meant no more than sharing a sandwich or a drink.

The secret, Randall thought, was to make sure the woman one was involved with was also involved with someone else. If she could manage to keep Pat as a lover, she'd be satisfied. She was beginning to realize that it might take some compromising to keep the status quo. . . . A child wouldn't have to tie her down. After all, she could hire a nurse just as Kenneth had suggested. And a kid might also keep Kenneth busy and off her back. Maybe he would enjoy fatherhood, even though she couldn't imagine herself as a mother. . . .

"What about the baby? You know how much I want that child," Kenneth was saying.

Randall saw her opportunity. "I never dreamed you'd actually run out and sue some woman whose greatest crime was allowing your wife to accompany her on a skiing trip. Honestly, Kenneth, you've really embarrassed me. She must think we're both crazy."

She took Kenneth's hand. "I'm hoping for a son."

"Do you really mean that?"

Kenneth had swallowed the hook. It only remained for her to reel him in.

"Of course I mean it. I'll be a loving mother, but I'll hire a nanny for the baby so I can be a working mother, too."

"What about Pat Martin? Do you intend to keep seeing her?"

"Not if you don't want me to. But honestly, Kenneth," she wheedled, "what damage does it do? I could understand your objections if I were involved with a man, but a woman? All we do is hold each other and exchange a few school girl kisses. You certainly can't be jealous of that? You're much too much of a man for that."

"I hope you mean what you're saying. I want us to get along, to have our own family."

"Give me the chance to show you."

Kenneth pulled Randall to him and kissed her roughly. The thought of her with a woman rather excited him.

"I guess I'd better go tell Margaret Bailey that I don't plan a suit against Dr. McKenzie. I wish you hadn't told her about it. I never intended to go through with it."

159

"I'm sorry, but you frightened me so. I didn't think."

"Do you want to come in with me and talk to her?"

"I'd rather not. Please take care of it for me. I'm a little sick to my stomach," she said with a smile. "Your son has given me a touch of morning sickness."

Kenneth walked toward his office feeling much calmer, relieved that Randall had believed his bluff — but slightly embarrassed that she had involved this McKenzie woman. The thought of going public with his private problems made him a little nauseous, too. If Randall knew him better, she'd have known that he would never take such personal matters near a courtroom.

I've gambled and won, he thought. She'd carry the baby to term. He would have someone to carry on his name. Even if the baby was a girl, she would keep her own name. He'd make her a partner in the firm when she grew up, the same as he would a son. He would have his child understand the value of the Grayson name.

Kenneth smiled, but the smile quickly decayed. He didn't like the idea that Randall was involved with someone else, not so much that there would be another person sharing her bed, but because his not knowing had made him feel like a fool. But then — wouldn't Paul Martin have a stroke if he knew his wife Patricia was playing doctor with Randall? Well, he wouldn't tell him. The knowledge gave him untold power over Randall. That was another reason to let them continue to play. If Randall lost interest and no longer cared what happened to Pat and Paul's marriage, or if he told Paul about the women, his power would be gone. He was determined to give Randall the impression that he would ignore her games with Pat as long as she was discreet with them. Now that he knew exactly what a school girl involvement it was and that Randall had no intention of leaving their marriage, he could tolerate it, control it. Perhaps he could even become part of the affair. . . .

He smiled genuinely as he placed his hand on the doorknob of his office. All in all this whole thing had put him in the cat-bird's seat.

"I apologize for keeping you ladies waiting. My wife is not well. This has been a difficult pregnancy for her already. At the moment she has very severe morning sickness. She joins me, however, in expressing our apologies to you, Dr. McKenzie. We both regret that a private and personal matter made its way into your life. I hope you'll accept my apology and my wife's."

Margaret nodded toward Megan.

"Of course. I'm just sorry the whole incident happened," Megan said graciously.

"I have a favor to ask of all three of you." Kenneth put on the boyish expression that had served him well in jury trials. "I would appreciate it if we kept this little conversation just between the four of us."

"You have our word," Margaret Bailey said. "It will go no further."

"Oh, one other thing, Ms. Bailey. I would appreciate it if you see that the tape of the incident is destroyed."

Margaret Bailey raised both hands. "I can't destroy the tape. As an attorney, you must understand that I have an obligation to protect my client. Should the incident ever be dredged up again, the tape might be needed. But I give you my personal assurance that the tape is in a very secure location. My client doesn't wish publicity any more than you do."

He got to his feet and extended his hand to all three women. "I thank you all for your understanding."

The women left, and Kenneth was once again alone in his office. He thought again of his new-found power over Randall, and he spoke his thoughts out loud. "Lesbian or not, Dr. McKenzie, you have my sincere thanks."

The women did not speak until they were sitting in Megan's car in the parking lot. As the doors of the Mercedes closed, all three looked at one another and broke into spontaneous laughter.

"If ever two people deserve each other, it's those two," Margaret managed to get out.

"Amen," Megan said between peals of laughter.

"Margaret, what tape is this that you have, and where is this secure vault you intend to keep it in?" Lynn wiped tears from her eyes.

"Attorneys sometimes have to improvise. There could have been a tape. Mr. Grayson considered it quite possible."

The laughter dissolved into smiles. Lynn reached over and patted Megan on the shoulder. "You're home safe, Meggie."

"Thanks to Margaret and you. You are one hell of an attorney, Margaret."

Lynn laughed. "She's one hell of a poker player. Remind me never to play cards with you, Margaret. You're much too good at bluffing."

"Justice is always a gamble when one bets on the law," Margaret said. "So, at times I help it along with creative disclosure."

Megan drove to Margaret's office building. "Thanks again, Margaret. Send me a bill and I'll get a check to you immediately."

"No charge. I'll take it out in EKGs if I ever have a heart problem. And speaking of heart problems, I'm not going to ask you if you ever were involved with Grayson's wife — that's none of my business. But, if you ever do get involved with a married woman, please make sure the charming couple is not another Bonnie and Clyde."

"You are looking at a much wiser woman," Megan assured her.

Chapter 37

Lynn was an even better skier than Megan and, if possible, even more fanatical about the sport. On Christmas morning they ate breakfast at the coffee shop and were on the ski lift by ten. It was colder than the previous day, but both women found the cold invigorating. They had been skiing for two hours when the accident happened. An unexpected rut, a touch of ice, and Lynn's skis went out from under her. Megan, behind her, watched helplessly as Lynn hit the ground. She knew by the way Lynn fell that she was hurt, and she was immediately at her side, getting off her skis, and kneeling to examine Lynn's leg.

Lynn's face was drawn with pain. "It's broken."

"Let me see." Megan looked at Lynn's leg. "You're right, it's broken."

"It hurts like hell."

"I'll use your ski for a splint." Megan worked quickly. "We're only five minutes from the ski patrol station. I'll get help and come right back. Will you be all right?"

"I don't think I'll freeze to death in ten minutes. And if no one skis over me while you're gone, I should be here when you get back."

"Do you think you could get down with just my help?" Megan asked anxiously. "You don't seem to be in too much pain."

Lynn's attempted laugh turned into a grimace. "If I could stand up right now, I'd kill you with my bare hands. I am in a great deal of pain. The only reason I'm not crying is that my tears would freeze in this weather. Now get the hell out of here and bring me someone who can get me to a real doctor."

Megan returned fifteen minutes later with a four-member emergency team. They gave Lynn an injection of morphine, resplinted her leg, placed her on a stretcher, and rushed her to a waiting ambulance at the foot of the mountain. Megan stayed at Lynn's side the entire way.

Three hours later Megan and Lynn were in a taxi heading for the lodge. Lynn's foot and leg had been placed in a plaster cast that stopped just below her knee and had a small heel allowing her to walk without crutches. When they reached the lodge, Lynn settled herself on the sofa with an extra pillow for her foot.

"Are you in a lot of pain?" Megan asked.

"Surprisingly, no. In fact, I'm hungry. Do you want to go out to eat? After all, it is Christmas."

"I have a better idea. You stay here and relax, and I'll bring Christmas dinner to you. What do you say to Louigi's veal marsala with mushrooms and a side order of spaghetti?"

"And some rum cheesecake," Lynn added.

"And some rum cheesecake." Megan shook her head. "How in the world do you stay thin? You eat like a Clydesdale."

"Nervous energy. I have a high metabolic rate."

"Good thing. You'd be a blimp if you didn't."

"Your bedside manner is charming. Enough of this harassment. Go out and gather Christmas dinner for your patient!"

"*My* patient! *You,* who wanted a real doctor."

"I was out of my head with pain. I didn't know what I was saying."

Megan got her coat and headed for the door.

"Don't forget the cheesecake!" Lynn shouted as the door closed.

Lynn ate everything on her plate plus Megan's leftover cheesecake. Megan cleared the dishes, got coffee, and started the VCR and the movie they had rented, "On Golden Pond."

"I love that movie more every time I see it," Lynn said as Megan rewound the tape and brought her more coffee. "I would like to grow old with someone I shared that kind of love with."

"Then you'd better learn to ski."

"Look who's talking. It seems I remember you with a cast on your leg about four years ago."

"I was tripped."

"Yes, by your own skis." Lynn smiled. "Seriously though, I think it would be wonderful to know someone that well for so long. Then again, it would be my luck that the bear who got the old lesbian in the move would get me too."

Megan added another log to the fire and turned to look out the large windows. The panes were crusted with a thin layer of ice that started in the corners like lace and formed a border that framed the night sky. It was snowing lightly and Megan watched as snowflakes were caught by the wind and blown in showers across her view. The fire crackled and popped as the new log started to burn.

Megan's eyes moved to Lynn, and she felt a new warmth inside herself. She was becoming more acutely aware of aspects of Lynn that she hadn't paid attention to before. She saw an attractive, intelligent woman with a razor-sharp wit and an exquisite sensitivity. Megan's eyes moved to the fire and back to Lynn. She felt warmed by both.

"Do you think I could get a ski to fit my cast?"

"Only if they're used to outfitting Big Foot."

"In that case, after you ski in the morning, the two of us can ride a snowmobile."

"Sounds good to me. But I think I'll skip skiing tomorrow. The snowmobile sounds like fun. We could go in the morning and make a day of it. There are some great runs around here."

"Okay. We'll need some sandwiches and a thermos of coffee to take along."

"God, do you ever stop thinking of your stomach?" Megan laughed. "We aren't going to Siberia."

"You're a wonderful nurse," Lynn teased. "Don't deny your patient nourishment."

"Gee, thanks. Your nurse thinks it's time for you to go to bed. I'll help you get up the stairs."

Lynn put her arm around Megan's shoulder and eased slowly up the steps. Megan left Lynn sitting on the side of her bed while she gathered the articles Lynn needed to get ready for sleep. She left Lynn and returned a half hour later to find Lynn already under the covers.

"Do you need anything else? I brought you water and a radio. I'll tune in an FM station so you can listen to Christmas music. I'll leave the door open and the hall light on. If you need me, just holler. I'm a very light sleeper."

"Thank you, Meggie," Lynn said softly. I'll see you in the morning."

Megan turned the light off in Lynn's room and returned to her own. She undressed and stepped into a warm shower. The water fell lightly over her shoulders and cascaded down her body. She lifted her face to the warmth and closed her eyes as the spray brushed against them. She turned and let the water roll down her back and legs. Her body relaxed to the warmth and constant beating rhythm, and she stood in its softness for a full ten minutes.

She wrapped a large white terry cloth towel around herself as she stepped out of the shower, and patted the water from her skin. Thoughts of Lynn filled her mind again, and Megan felt excitement move through her. She sat on the edge of her bed, still patting her skin with the softness of the towel. She felt an overwhelming desire to feel Lynn's body next to her own, to feel Lynn's lips on hers, to make love with Lynn. She had become gradually aware over the past few weeks that she was in love with Lynn, and now she was certain that she wanted a life with her — a full commitment.

Megan laid the towel on the bed and walked slowly toward Lynn's room. The dim light in the hallway outlined her trim, naked body as she moved. She entered the bedroom slowly, and Lynn awakened from a light sleep.

"Megan, what's wrong?" She saw the outline of Megan's body as she moved toward her.

"Nothing is wrong." Megan spoke softly as she lifted the blanket and sheet and slid into bed with Lynn. She took Lynn's face in her hands and kissed her gently. The hall light outlined Megan's face as she smiled into Lynn's eyes and whispered, "I love you, Lynn. I want to make love with you."

Lynn put her arms around Megan and drew her body closer. She stroked her face lightly as she kissed Megan's forehead, her eyes, her mouth. Her heart pounded as she felt the warm welcome of Megan's tongue. Her hands explored the warm softness of Megan's skin and felt the excitement of desire move through her body.

Megan moved with exquisite slowness as she lowered her body onto Lynn's. She felt the firmness of Lynn's nipples against her own and lightly moved her breasts over the soft skin. Her open lips brushed Lynn's as she moved her tongue gently inside Lynn's mouth.

"I love you, Megan," Lynn spoke into Megan's mouth. "I want you very much." She looked into Megan's eyes. "But there is something you need to know."

"What is it?" Megan's voice was filled with concern.

"You're killing my leg."

Megan shifted her weight. "I'm sorry. Why didn't you say something?"

"I thought I was dreaming and the pain would go away."

They both laughed.

Lynn brushed Megan's face with her fingertips. "I'd hoped that the first time we made love would be filled with romance." She smiled. "But I hadn't planned on a broken leg."

"Do you want me to leave?" Megan teased.

"Do you want to see a grown woman cry? We'll manage despite the cast."

Megan felt Lynn's hand move to her breast, and desire coursed through her.

Lynn pulled Megan closer. Her kisses were slow and deep. Her hand caressed Megan's breasts. Her touch was gentle as she trailed her fingers along the soft curves of Megan's body, lingering, caressing, appreciating the beauty she held. Warm kisses found Megan's neck and shoulders and returned again to her lips.

Megan felt the tender touch of Lynn's tongue as it moved leisurely inside her mouth, stroking and caressing, deepening the desire already in her. Her body trembled slightly as she felt Lynn's hand glide gently between her thighs. She moved her body to meet Lynn's touch as fingers moved in the wetness and stroked the satin softness. Megan's pleasure was like a flame. It grew brighter and stronger with every stroke.

Lynn's mouth grew more insistent, and Megan matched her intensity, sucking her tongue, pulling it farther and farther inside.

Megan gasped as Lynn's fingers entered her and began a rhythmic motion that fanned the flames of her desire. She pushed down, bringing Lynn deeper within herself. Pleasure flooded her body and became her only reality. Pleasure created by Lynn's touch, Lynn's love. She pressed her fingers into Lynn's back as a flood of sensation carried her trembling into ecstasy. Her mouth pressed hard against Lynn's lips, tears filled her eyes, and her body stiffened. She melted and flowed into Lynn.

Lynn was kissing her again. Tender kisses. Kisses on her eyes, her cheeks, herr lips. Warm kisses, speaking love. Hot kisses, speaking desire. The radio was spilling Christmas music into the room, the mellow sounds of White Christmas in contrast to the wind outside the lodge, whistling and shrieking as it whipped around the mountain and rattled the windows of the bedroom, the tinkling sound adding to the soft Christmas music.

Megan held Lynn's face between her hands, and her lips moved with a feather's lightness on Lynn's mouth, her tongue seeking Lynn's with a gentle touch. She was electrified by her own desire — a desire to bring pleasure to Lynn. Her mouth caressed Lynn's breasts. Lingering kisses that took joy in the firm nipples and soft fullness they found. Joyful kisses speaking longing and promising fulfillment. Hot kisses as they met Lynn's thighs and breathed in the sweet scent of her cologne. Her skin was soft and yielding beneath Megan's lips.

More yielding still, the wet satin that met her tongue as she stroked the secret place between Lynn's thighs. The taste was clean and salty on her lips and tongue, and she sighed with joy as she discovered its wonders. Fantastic wonders — all soft and warm and satin. The textures played like music in her mouth, and she dedicated herself to their song. Her mouth moved like a fine bow calling forth a symphony of sensations within Lynn. Movement and sensations building to a grand crescendo, overwhelming Lynn's body with unadulterated ecstasy. Her pleasure spoken in a long, deep murmuring sound born deep within her soul.

Lynn pulled Megan gently to her, lifting her face to meet her mouth. Surrounding it with lover's kisses, seeking home within its lips. Her arms enfolded Megan, and she felt Megan's heart pounding against her own.

They heard the sound of their own warm breathing, made more clear by the cry of the frigid wind moving fiercely outside their room. The light from the hallway highlighted their bodies and glinted off the love in their eyes.

"I love you, Meggie," Lynn whispered into Megan's dark hair. "I wish I could tell you how much."

Megan lifted her head and looked lovingly into Lynn's eyes.

"I'm awfully glad you do." Megan kissed her eyes with infinite tenderness. Her kisses moved to Lynn's mouth — tender at first — growing more intense. Her nipples brushed against Lynn's breasts and Lynn felt her desire burn again. She pressed her lips intently on Megan's and sought the softness of her tongue.

"I want you in my mouth," she spoke into Megan's lips. "Come over me, Meggie."

Megan knelt over Lynn and lowered herself within inches of Lynn's mouth. She felt Lynn's hands move under her and cradle the soft roundness of her hips.

"You're beautiful. So very, very beautiful," Lynn said as she pulled Megan gently to her mouth.

Megan moaned quietly as she felt Lynn's warm breath and soft tongue rise to meet her. She closed her eyes as the soft strokes and gentle sucking motion pushed and pulled her from one pleasure to another. Desire filled her completely as passion flared to untouched heights and ignited an orgasmic fire that consumed her totally. Her hands clasped the headboard as her body shuddered with pleasure. She heard a low moan, a sharp cry, a scream. It blended with the wind's cry and moved about the room as the wind screamed outside.

She lay in Lynn's arms, relaxed and warm, her head on Lynn's shoulder. Their bodies rose and fell together as their breathing became synchronized.

"I love you, Meggie. 'Your eyes have shot their arrows into my heart.' " Lynn kissed Megan's hair and caressed it with her hand.

Megan lifted her head and looked at Lynn. Tears had left wet traces on her cheeks. "I love *you*, Lynn Bradley. I'm a pushover for a woman who can quote Dante."

Lynn grinned. "I wish I had known that sooner. I would have memorized the entire *Divine Comedy*."

They fell asleep to the sounds of *Silent Night* and the comfort of each other's touch.

A few of the publications of
THE NAIAD PRESS, INC.
P.O. Box 10543 ● Tallahassee, Florida 32302
Phone (904) 539-9322
Mail orders welcome. Please include 15% postage.

CHERISHED LOVE by Evelyn Kennedy. 192 pp. Erotic
Lesbian love story.   ISBN 0-941483-08-8 $8.95

LAST SEPTEMBER by Helen R. Hull. 208 pp. Six stories & a
glorious novella.   ISBN 0-941483-09-6   8.95

THE SECRET IN THE BIRD by Camarin Grae. 312 pp. Striking,
psychological suspense novel.   ISBN 0-941483-05-3   8.95

TO THE LIGHTNING by Catherine Ennis. 208 pp. Romantic
Lesbian 'Robinson Crusoe' adventure.   ISBN 0-941483-06-1   8.95

THE OTHER SIDE OF VENUS by Shirley Verel. 224 pp.
Luminous, romantic love story.   ISBN 0-941483-07-X   8.95

DREAMS AND SWORDS by Katherine V. Forrest. 192 pp.
Romantic, erotic, imaginative stories. ISBN 0-941483-03-7   8.95

MEMORY BOARD by Jane Rule. 336 pp. Memorable novel
about an aging Lesbian couple.   ISBN 0-941483-02-9   8.95

THE ALWAYS ANONYMOUS BEAST by Lauren Wright
Douglas. 224 pp. A Caitlin Reese mystery. First in a series.
                                       ISBN 0-941483-04-5   8.95

SEARCHING FOR SPRING by Patricia A. Murphy. 224 pp.
Novel about the recovery of love.   ISBN 0-941483-00-2   8.95

DUSTY'S QUEEN OF HEARTS DINER by Lee Lynch. 240 pp.
Romantic blue-collar novel.   ISBN 0-941483-01-0   8.95

PARENTS MATTER by Ann Muller. 240 pp. Parents'
relationships with Lesbian daughters and gay sons.
                                       ISBN 0-930044-91-6   9.95

THE PEARLS by Shelley Smith. 176 pp. Passion and fun in
the Caribbean sun.   ISBN 0-930044-93-2   7.95

MAGDALENA by Sarah Aldridge. 352 pp. Epic Lesbian novel
set on three continents.   ISBN 0-930044-99-1   8.95

THE BLACK AND WHITE OF IT by Ann Allen Shockley.
144 pp. Short stories.   ISBN 0-930044-96-7   7.95

SAY JESUS AND COME TO ME by Ann Allen Shockley. 288
pp. Contemporary romance.   ISBN 0-930044-98-3   8.95

LOVING HER by Ann Allen Shockley. 192 pp. Romantic love
story.   ISBN 0-930044-97-5   7.95

MURDER AT THE NIGHTWOOD BAR by Katherine V. Forrest. 240 pp. A Kate Delafield mystery. Second in a series.
ISBN 0-930044-92-4   8.95

ZOE'S BOOK by Gail Pass. 224 pp. Passionate, obsessive love story.
ISBN 0-930044-95-9   7.95

WINGED DANCER by Camarin Grae. 228 pp. Erotic Lesbian adventure story.
ISBN 0-930044-88-6   8.95

PAZ by Camarin Grae. 336 pp. Romantic Lesbian adventurer with the power to change the world.
ISBN 0-930044-89-4   8.95

SOUL SNATCHER by Camarin Grae. 224 pp. A puzzle, an adventure, a mystery — Lesbian romance.
ISBN 0-930044-90-8   8.95

THE LOVE OF GOOD WOMEN by Isabel Miller. 224 pp. Long-awaited new novel by the author of the beloved *Patience and Sarah*.
ISBN 0-930044-81-9   8.95

THE HOUSE AT PELHAM FALLS by Brenda Weathers. 240 pp. Suspenseful Lesbian ghost story.
ISBN 0-930044-79-7   7.95

HOME IN YOUR HANDS by Lee Lynch. 240 pp. More stories from the author of *Old Dyke Tales*.
ISBN 0-930044-80-0   7.95

EACH HAND A MAP by Anita Skeen. 112 pp. Real-life poems that touch us all.
ISBN 0-930044-82-7   6.95

SURPLUS by Sylvia Stevenson. 342 pp. A classic early Lesbian novel.
ISBN 0-930044-78-9   6.95

PEMBROKE PARK by Michelle Martin. 256 pp. Derring-do and daring romance in Regency England.
ISBN 0-930044-77-0   7.95

THE LONG TRAIL by Penny Hayes. 248 pp. Vivid adventures of two women in love in the old west.
ISBN 0-930044-76-2   8.95

HORIZON OF THE HEART by Shelley Smith. 192 pp. Hot romance in summertime New England.
ISBN 0-930044-75-4   7.95

AN EMERGENCE OF GREEN by Katherine V. Forrest. 288 pp. Powerful novel of sexual discovery.
ISBN 0-930044-69-X   8.95

THE LESBIAN PERIODICALS INDEX edited by Claire Potter. 432 pp. Author & subject index.
ISBN 0-930044-74-6   29.95

DESERT OF THE HEART by Jane Rule. 224 pp. A classic; basis for the movie *Desert Hearts*.
ISBN 0-930044-73-8   7.95

SPRING FORWARD/FALL BACK by Sheila Ortiz Taylor. 288 pp. Literary novel of timeless love.
ISBN 0-930044-70-3   7.95

FOR KEEPS by Elisabeth Nonas. 144 pp. Contemporary novel about losing and finding love.
ISBN 0-930044-71-1   7.95

TORCHLIGHT TO VALHALLA by Gale Wilhelm. 128 pp. Classic novel by a great Lesbian writer.
ISBN 0-930044-68-1   7.95

LESBIAN NUNS: BREAKING SILENCE edited by Rosemary Curb and Nancy Manahan. 432 pp. Unprecedented autobiographies of religious life.
ISBN 0-930044-62-2   9.95

YANTRAS OF WOMANLOVE by Tee A. Corinne. 64 pp.
Photos by noted Lesbian photographer. ISBN 0-930044-30-4 6.95

MRS. PORTER'S LETTER by Vicki P. McConnell. 224 pp.
The first Nyla Wade mystery. ISBN 0-930044-29-0 7.95

TO THE CLEVELAND STATION by Carol Anne Douglas.
192 pp. Interracial Lesbian love story. ISBN 0-930044-27-4 6.95

THE NESTING PLACE by Sarah Aldridge. 224 pp. A
three-woman triangle—love conquers all! ISBN 0-930044-26-6 7.95

THIS IS NOT FOR YOU by Jane Rule. 284 pp. A letter to a
beloved is also an intricate novel. ISBN 0-930044-25-8 8.95

FAULTLINE by Sheila Ortiz Taylor. 140 pp. Warm, funny,
literate story of a startling family. ISBN 0-930044-24-X 6.95

THE LESBIAN IN LITERATURE by Barbara Grier. 3d ed.
Foreword by Maida Tilchen. 240 pp. Comprehensive bibliography.
Literary ratings; rare photos. ISBN 0-930044-23-1 7.95

ANNA'S COUNTRY by Elizabeth Lang. 208 pp. A woman
finds her Lesbian identity. ISBN 0-930044-19-3 6.95

PRISM by Valerie Taylor. 158 pp. A love affair between two
women in their sixties. ISBN 0-930044-18-5 6.95

BLACK LESBIANS: AN ANNOTATED BIBLIOGRAPHY
compiled by J. R. Roberts. Foreword by Barbara Smith. 112 pp.
Award-winning bibliography. ISBN 0-930044-21-5 5.95

THE MARQUISE AND THE NOVICE by Victoria Ramstetter.
108 pp. A Lesbian Gothic novel. ISBN 0-930044-16-9 4.95

OUTLANDER by Jane Rule. 207 pp. Short stories and essays
by one of our finest writers. ISBN 0-930044-17-7 6.95

SAPPHISTRY: THE BOOK OF LESBIAN SEXUALITY by
Pat Califia. 2d edition, revised. 195 pp. ISBN 0-9330044-47-9 7.95

ALL TRUE LOVERS by Sarah Aldridge. 292 pp. Romantic
novel set in the 1930s and 1940s. ISBN 0-930044-10-X 7.95

A WOMAN APPEARED TO ME by Renee Vivien. 65 pp. A
classic; translated by Jeannette H. Foster. ISBN 0-930044-06-1 5.00

CYTHEREA'S BREATH by Sarah Aldridge. 240 pp. Romantic
novel about women's entrance into medicine.
  ISBN 0-930044-02-9 6.95

TOTTIE by Sarah Aldridge. 181 pp. Lesbian romance in the
turmoil of the sixties. ISBN 0-930044-01-0 6.95

THE LATECOMER by Sarah Aldridge. 107 pp. A delicate love
story. ISBN 0-930044-00-2 5.00

ODD GIRL OUT by Ann Bannon.	ISBN 0-930044-83-5	5.95
I AM A WOMAN by Ann Bannon.	ISBN 0-930044-84-3	5.95
WOMEN IN THE SHADOWS by Ann Bannon.	ISBN 0-930044-85-1	5.95
JOURNEY TO A WOMAN by Ann Bannon.	ISBN 0-930044-86-X	5.95
BEEBO BRINKER by Ann Bannon.	ISBN 0-930044-87-8	5.95

Legendary novels written in the fifties and sixties,
set in the gay mecca of Greenwich Village.

VOLUTE BOOKS

JOURNEY TO FULFILLMENT	Early classics by Valerie	3.95
A WORLD WITHOUT MEN	Taylor: The Erika Frohmann	3.95
RETURN TO LESBOS	series.	3.95

These are just a few of the many Naiad Press titles — we are the oldest and largest lesbian/feminist publishing company in the world. Please request a complete catalog. We offer personal service; we encourage and welcome direct mail orders from individuals who have limited access to bookstores carrying our publications.